Firecrackered

An Essie Cobb Senior Sleuth Mystery

by

Patricia Rockwell

For information, email Cozy Cat Press, cozycatpress@aol.com or visit our website at: www.cozycatpress.com

COZY CAT
PRESS

ISBN: 978-1-939816-89-4
Printed in the United States of America

Cover design by Rick Forgus
http://www.atomicwerewolfstudio.com/

10 9 8 7 6 5 4 3 2 1

This book is dedicated to all the senior sleuths out there. May you all find what you're looking for!

Chapter 1

Essie Cobb diligently crunched down on a little carrot stick from her summer salad, as she ran her fork through the pieces of lettuce looking for hidden slices of radish. They always managed to sneak in among the other vegetables because of their translucent demeanor––they were truly the cruciferous villains of the salad world. Essie hated radishes and wasted no time in ousting the little rascals from her bowl.

"Essie!" called her tablemate Marjorie, "I asked what you're wearing on the Fourth."

Essie raised her sparkling head of silver curls and stared at Marjorie through her wire-rimmed glasses. "I'm sure I'll think of something before the holiday, Marjorie," she said smugly.

"I like to give lots of thought to my holiday outfits," said the sprightly redhead in retort, "and, besides, I really want to win the prize."

"Prize," scoffed Opal, Essie's tablemate on her other side. "They'll probably just give it to the most outlandish costume. That's what they usually do. The louder, the better." She jutted out her chin and pulled on her opal necklace, a nervous habit that everyone recognized as uniquely Opal.

"Not necessarily, Opal," said Essie, her blue eyes twinkling. "Hilda Sweeny won best costume last year if I remember correctly. I thought her outfit was dull as dishwater."

"It was very stylish," said the pert and perky Marjorie. "I, for one, intend to make my costume one I would not be embarrassed to wear outside of Happy Haven."

"Are you suggesting," said Essie, her cheeks now taking on the pink color that so often infused her features, "that *my* costumes are embarrassing?"

"Essie," said Opal in a whisper over her shoulder to her companion, "as you virtually *never* go anywhere outside of Happy Haven, I believe Marjorie has a point."

"Oh hoops and humdingers!" cried Essie, "it's a *costume* contest. I'm not going to wear a bag. I'm going to dress up in something colorful. And as it's a Fourth of July costume contest, I'm going to dress as something appropriately patriotic."

At that point, Santos, their regular waiter was gathering up their empty salad plates and placing their entrees in front of them. All of the ladies gave little shouts of glee as Santos deposited their favorite dish— chicken pot pies. The tiny pastries simply glistened with savory goodness.

"Miss Essie," said the young man as he lifted Essie's salad dish to his rolling cart, "you no like the radishes?"

"I like them just fine, Santos," declared Essie. "I enjoy searching for them and then hiding them on one side of the bowl so I won't have to eat them. I consider it a game between me and your salad chef back there."

"We can fix you salad with no radish," suggested Santos.

"No!" said Essie. "I don't want any special treatment. I prefer to figure out such problems for myself. Besides, I like to work for my chicken pie." She gave Santos one of her sweetest smiles.

"Oh, for heaven's sake, Essie," chided Marjorie. "She's teasing you, Santos. You don't need to make a special salad just for her. One day she eats radishes and the next day, she doesn't. She's ninety. What can you expect?"

"You can expect that I will change my mind," snapped Essie. "So get used to it." Santos smiled with a little cringe and headed back into the kitchen.

"Really, Essie," sighed Opal, patting her neat grey bun. "You rattle that poor boy. He's just trying to do his job. And you're not that much older than the *rest* of us anyway. I'm almost ninety—just two more years."

"Speak for yourself, Opal," said Marjorie, cheerfully. "I'm eighty-six. I'm *much* younger than all of you." She shook her reddish-brown curls vigorously.

"We can't say that for certain. You might *not* be the youngest of us all," said Essie. "Don't forget. There's Fay." She crossed her arms and nodded across the table to the chubby little lady sitting in a wheel chair. Fay's face appeared lost in a dream, her spoon full of chicken pie lolling upside down in her mouth. All three of the women suddenly stared at her. Fay had the look of an ageless waif. Her short, chopped light brown hair jutted out every which way, with little wisps curling around the tops of her ears. Fay, realizing that she was the center of attention, slowly removed the spoon from her mouth and smiled.

"We don't know how old she is," said Marjorie.

"She's probably younger than all of us," said Opal.

"Or older," said Essie. Fay frowned.

"We'll never know, because she'll never tell," said Marjorie. It was true. Fay, dear and sweet as she was, never spoke. She giggled, smiled, and often appeared to be listening and responding. The women knew she had remarkable computer skills and had at one time in her life been a librarian. Why she was, for all intents and purposes, now mute, they had no idea. They only knew that she was their tablemate and friend and they loved her and involved her in all of their activities.

At that moment, a tall slender gentleman, dressed in a pale blue-striped seersucker suit, appeared behind Opal.

"Opal?" he said quizzically, so softly it was almost a whisper. Opal turned to see who had spoken, if someone had spoken at all.

"Oh my!" she said, "Mr. Mills! I had no idea you were here. Are you visiting someone? Are you a resident?"

"Yes, I'm a resident," the slender man replied. "I had no idea you were either. I've lived here several weeks now. We must eat in different shifts. I usually eat in the later time period." There were so many residents at the Happy Haven Retirement Center that the dining hall could not accommodate all of the guests in one sitting, so residents ate at different times.

"What prompts you to be dining at this time tonight?" asked Opal.

"Oh, a little something special. . ." he said, waving his hand in dismissal of her question. "How long have you lived here, Opal?"

"Oh, my goodness," Opal replied. "Years! Or I should say, about twelve years. Oh, how thoughtless of me. Mr. Mills . . ."

"Lester. Please. Call me Lester."

"Lester, I'd like to introduce my table companions. Marjorie, Essie, and Fay." Opal pointed out each woman who nodded as she was introduced.

"Delighted to meet you all," he replied, glancing at each woman, but his gaze hardly leaving Opal's face. "I must say, Opal, I had no idea I'd find you *here*. I assumed you'd still be Terrence Brandt's right-hand girl. He always spoke of you so highly. Said he could never find anything without you there. He even said you could run that tax firm of his all by yourself and he could go on vacation for months and no one would miss him. . ."

"Oh, that's so sweet . . . but, of course, he was just being kind." She lifted her shoulders in a way that Essie recognized as the closest Opal ever came to flirting.

"I can't believe you're even old enough to *retire*," the man continued, "let alone be living here in a retirement facility. You really look wonderful, Opal. I hope we'll be able to 'socialize' sometime. That's the main reason I moved here. When I originally retired, I just stayed at home in my big old house and let my staff take care of me, but I was so bored and lonely. Moving into Happy Haven was the best thing I've ever done. It's invigorated me. I'd love to just sit down with you and talk about old times."

"Oh, Opal loves to talk about old times," gushed Marjorie, smiling coquettishly at the attractive silver-headed gentleman. "We *all* do."

"I, ah, hear that Happy Haven sets up seating for the residents to watch the city fireworks display on the Fourth . . ." he began.

"Yes. They do," agreed Opal, her grey-blue eyes glittering.

"It's a very romantic event," added Marjorie, again fluttering her eyelashes aggressively at the man. "A warm July night, fireflies popping alight all over . . ."

"Yes," added Essie, with more practical information. "They set out lawn chairs and the residents can watch the display from our front lawn. The city sets off the fireworks at the City Park which is just down the hill to the east."

"That sounds lovely!" said Lester. "Perhaps you would join me on the front lawn for the evening, Opal?" He looked down shyly, and then peeked at her over the tops of his horn-rimmed eyeglasses.

"I . . . I . . ." muttered Opal, "well, I guess, yes, I would like that. We could catch up on old times." She blushed profusely as she accepted the invitation and Lester beamed, never taking his eyes off of her face.

At that moment, some raucous rock music erupted from the loud speaker system. Essie caught some of the lyrics—something about *Michelle Pfeiffer*. Some of the ladies held their hands over their ears, but everyone looked around to see why this music, so uncharacteristic of senior citizens, was playing. Suddenly, one gentleman rose up from his seat at one of the tables and walked directly to the center of the room. Slowly, he began moving his hips in time to the music as he looked around at the many ladies still seated at their tables. Within a few seconds, two more gentlemen stood up and glided over to stand next to the man in the center. In perfect harmony, the two joined him with identical movements. All three men worked together like one unit as they looked around with sly smiles on their faces at the ladies in the room. Then, two more men joined in—one even with his walker. Then two more.

At Essie's table, Lester Mills said, "Oops, my turn. Sorry, ladies. Have to go!" Then he also joined the growing group of male dancers in the middle of the dining hall. "What is that awful music?" asked Opal after Lester had departed.

"Oh, that's Bruno Mars' 'Uptown Funk,'" answered Marjorie, nodding her head in time to the music. Essie found her foot tapping in spite of herself, and suddenly the music exploded with massive drum-beats, and the men were flinging their arms about and gyrating around like striptease dancers. A few of the more daring women in the room removed loose pieces of clothing such as scarves and hankies and flung them at the men. The women began to shout, "Go, Bill!" or "Take it off,

Clyde!" as the men's dance increased in fury and frenzy. The women were now clapping in time to the music and even the kitchen staff had come out to see what was going on, and they too were joining in, clapping and stomping their feet. Other residents and staff had arrived from the lobby, and the dining room was packed to the gills with shouting and singing and hand-clapping. As the music built to a crescendo, the dancers swirled around faster and faster and then it all ended in one final pose when the music finally stopped.

When it was clear that the dance was over, the entire dining room broke into massive applause and shouting. The dancers bowed—all huffing and puffing, but noticeably proud. It was clear that the old men had enjoyed performing as much as the audience had enjoyed seeing them dance. With a nod from the first dancer who was probably the captain, the men jogged out of the dining room as well as eighty and ninety-year-old men can jog, and off into the lobby (and probably back to their own apartments to collapse and apply ice packs to appropriate body parts). The noise in the dining room began to settle.

At Essie's table, the four gal pals were still in a high state. Marjorie was cheering and waving her scarf.

"Oh, my! That was fabulous!" she cried. "Didn't you love it, Opal?"

"I thought it was energetic, but not terribly appropriate for senior citizens." Opal sneered and placed her hands sedately in her lap.

"Not even getting to see your new *beau* Lester move those hips?" teased Marjorie.

"Now, Marjorie," said Essie, calmly. "Not everyone is as progressive as you."

"That's true," acknowledged Marjorie. "What did you think, Fay?" With this question obviously directed at her, Fay giggled from her wheelchair and smiled.

"It *was* a catchy tune," agreed Opal.

"Indeed," said Essie. "I was so surprised when they just popped up all over the place and started dancing. That was strange."

"It's called a flash mob," explained Marjorie. "They do them in shopping malls, airports—all sorts of public places."

"But how do they prepare them?" asked Opal. "I mean, they must have to rehearse, don't they?"

"True," said Marjorie. "They must have been practicing somewhere."

"All of them?" asked Essie. "That dance must have included all the men at Happy Haven. I don't see how they could have gotten all of them together in one spot at one time to practice."

"Yes," argued Opal. "Just when would they have done that?"

"Well, they did!" proclaimed Marjorie. "And *all* the men at Happy Haven isn't that many. As you all know, women outnumber men here . . ."

"Eight to one!" answered Essie and Opal together as if on cue. This ratio was a selling point to incoming male residents and information the administration tried to *keep* from incoming female residents. Even so, the number was quite obvious to anyone just by looking around Happy Haven at the center's population.

"So it would be easier to gather the men together because there are fewer of them," continued Marjorie. She glanced over at Fay who was tapping her hands on the arms of her wheelchair and nodding her head back and forth in time to the rhythm of the song from the dance routine.

"Well, one thing we know for sure about Fay," observed Essie. "She may not talk, but she's not deaf."

"A deaf person would have heard *that* music," declared Opal.

Chapter 2

Essie rolled her walker back to her apartment down a long hallway on the first floor of Happy Haven. Despite her age, she moved fast. She knew that many people thought that using a walker meant moving slower for most elderly people, but not for Essie. When she'd first gotten her trusty metal charger, she'd felt like she could go a hundred miles an hour. It was almost as if her walker had a mind of its own and once Essie placed her fingers around the handles, it just took off. Now, rolling back down the hallway, in spite of herself, she was still humming that "Uptown Funky" song that the men had danced to in the dining room. Essie's shoulders moved up and down in time to the jaunty tune.

She reached her room and glanced with apprehension at her door. She knew she needed to get busy on her door decoration for the Fourth of July decorating contest. She had a vague idea of what she wanted to do, but still hadn't managed to mesh any of her thoughts together. She reached out and turned the door knob (no one locked their doors at Happy Haven unless they were going to be gone overnight). Scooting her walker inside, she rolled over to her favorite rocker and plopped down.

Soon, the apartment door opened and a large woman dressed in a nurse's uniform entered, laughing.

"Miss Essie! Lord almighty! Did you see them men?" she asked, dropping a clipboard and a tray of medicines on Essie's kitchen counter.

"You were there, Lorena?" asked Essie.

"I wouldn't have missed it for the world! I been watchin' 'em practice."

"Why didn't you tell me about it?" demanded Essie. "How did they ever keep that secret?"

"Oh, those men, they much more secretive than you ladies," replied the friendly aide. "You ready for your meds? Or you want to relax a bit after all that . . . *stimulation* . . . if you know what I mean?" She winked at Essie and walked over to where Essie was sitting.

"Really, Lorena," huffed Essie. "Those men are all too puny to do any *stimulating* . . . if you know what *I* mean."

"I thought they was cute," said Lorena with a suggestive little wiggle of her rear.

"Oh, posh tosh," sneered Essie, pointing to the sink. "Go on, give me my meds. Then you can help me get ready for bed."

"Whatever you say, missy," said Lorena with a little nod of her head. She headed back to the sink and returned with a glass of water and a small paper cup containing several pills. Essie downed them all at once and then took a slug of water. "There you go!" Lorena said, returning the glass to the counter. She came back to Essie.

"So, you were watching the men practice for that . . . uh, dance?" Essie asked.

"They call it a flash mob, Miss Essie."

"So I heard. Maybe because it's just a mob of people and it all happens in a flash," mused Essie as Lorena helped her to stand up.

"I think it's 'cause it's like this mob sort of appears in a flash out of nowhere . . . or that's what they want it to look like. You know, like they all just had this idea to dance all of a sudden and they all just happened to be there." Essie pushed her walker towards her bedroom with Lorena following. She guided herself towards her bed and sat down. "So, what nightie tonight?" Lorena asked.

"Just get me that blue one hanging on the hook inside my closet," ordered Essie, and Lorena grabbed the garment. She returned and started to help Essie out of her daytime outfit.

"I'm sure if we women put our minds to it, we could create a dance much more inventive than that . . . that *burly-que* the men did. I mean, you said you watched them practice. Just how often did they? I mean, practice."

"Oh, I have no idea. I just popped in once to the exercise room one afternoon when they was all up there and they was really going at it. I bet they had more fun planning it than actually doing it." Essie held her arms up and Lorena slid the nightie over her head. She stepped out of her brassiere which was now lying on the ground at her feet along with her trousers and Lorena bent over and picked up the items and placed them on the hook inside the closet.

"Here's your robe, sweetie," declared Lorena as she grabbed Essie's robe from the back of an arm chair and helped Essie into it. "Whatcha wanna do now?"

"I'm going to go back out to the living room and work on my puzzles," said Essie, grabbing her walker and guiding it firmly back to her recliner. She plopped down and grabbed a paperback book from the nearby end table.

"You still workin' on this mornin's puzzle?" asked Lorena.

"Yes. I didn't finish it. Kind of got busy thinking about decorating my door . . ."

"Your door? Oh, you mean for the Fourth? I know all you ladies really go all out on that door contest, don't you? The men don't seem to get into it so much . . ."

"They're probably much too busy practicing their erotic dancing," said Essie *sotto voce*.

Lorena laughed. "Now, Miss Essie, you just flummoxed that those men surprised you like that," said Lorena. "It's usually you ladies who do the surprising. You ladies always coming up with something clever or smart, and the men—they just sit there and shrug."

"That's true," said Essie with a firm nod. "I'm sure with the number of women here at Happy Haven . . ."

"Yes, eight to one over the men," said Lorena, reminding her with a finger wagging.

"Umm, yes; we're definitely in the majority."

"You could organize it, Miss Essie," said Lorena, "if anyone could."

"Oh, I don't know. I have a lot to do right now with getting my door decorated . . . and creating my costume . . . and, well . . . I just have a lot to do." Essie snuggled down into her recliner and picked up the pencil which she used as a book mark to keep her place in her puzzle book. She stared intently at the crossword puzzle on the page where the pencil was located. "Hmm, a five-letter-word for *overly romantic*."

"Got me, sweetie," said Lorena with a shrug. "I can't imagine anyone being *too* romantic for me." She waddled over to the kitchen counter and straightened up some unwashed dishes in the sink.

"Lorena!" Essie called, lifting her head from her puzzle.

"Yes?"

"Do me a favor, will you?"

"Of course, Essie. What is it?"

"Go sit on my toilet."

"What?"

"Go sit on my toilet."

"But, Essie, I don't have to use the bathroom right now."

"I don't want you to *use* it. I just want you to sit on it."

"Why?"

"Do I have to explain everything? Can't you just do it for me and I'll explain afterwards?"

"Oh, for heaven's sake!" cried Lorena, staring at Essie, expecting her to explain, but Essie just glared at her aide and nodded at the bathroom down the short hallway. Lorena sighed deeply and then with a distinct sneer headed back to the bathroom. She entered the small room and stood partially in the doorway, scowling at Essie who simply scowled back at her. Finally, Lorena went inside and shut the door. Several seconds later, she emerged and walked back to Essie.

"All right, Essie. I sat on your toilet. Are you happy?"

"Was it slippery?" asked Essie coyly from her recliner.

"What do you mean was it slippery? Was what slippery, Essie?"

"I mean was the toilet seat slippery?"

"You mean wet?"

"No, Lorena. Not wet slippery. I mean did it slip and slide around?"

"No, it's perfectly tightly attached."

Essie stared back at Lorena and then suddenly looked down at her lap with a frown.

"That will never do," she mumbled to herself. "It needs to be slippery."

"What are you talking about, Essie?" demanded Lorena, hands on her hips.

"I need a new toilet seat."

"No you don't. The one you have is perfectly fine."

"But it wouldn't *be* fine if it became loose and started to slip and slide, now, would it?" offered Essie.

Lorena shook her head and let out a large huff of air. "My goodness, Essie, I am totally confused. What are you talking about? What's wrong with your toilet seat and why do you think you need a new one?"

"Oh, I don't *need* a new one, but I want a new one. That's the problem. They won't give me a new one just because I want it. I'll have to convince them that I need it. And if it slips and slides around, then it wouldn't be safe for me to sit on and they'd have to replace it. Don't you see?"

"Oh, I see!" cried Lorena. "I see that you're nuts, old lady. Excuse me, Essie. I know I shouldn't say that, but what.....?"

"Lorena, I'm not nuts. I know what I'm doing. Suffice it to say that I want a new toilet seat for a very good reason, but to get one, I'll have to convince management that my present seat is defective and dangerous, so I'm asking your help to convince them that it's loose and that I slip when I sit on it. Can you help me?"

"You want me to lie for you?"

"Well," she said, scrunching her shoulders and her cheeks together, "I was hoping that you'd find the seat a little slippery and not have to lie. Actually, I pulled and prodded at it earlier today thinking I could loosen it, but I don't think I did a very good job and . . ."

"You want a new toilet seat and you want to make your present seat seem defective so you can convince our handyman to replace it?"

"In a nutshell," said Essie. She gave her aide her best guilty face.

"Oh, for heaven's sake," declared Lorena, heading back to the bathroom. She entered the room and Essie heard her grunting and mumbling. When she returned, she said, "There you go, Essie. I think you will find your toilet seat much too *slippery* now to sit on safely.

If I were you, I'd contact the front desk and demand the handyman come and replace it *asap* so you don't slide right into the bowl and get yourself flushed away."

"Oh, thank you, Lorena," said Essie. She started to extricate herself from her recliner but Lorena held up her hand. Bending down, she gave Essie a brief hug and headed towards the front door.

"Never a dull day at Happy Haven, I always say. Essie, you are a crackerjack."

"Bye, Lorena," said Essie sweetly, waving coyly to her aide as she disappeared out the door.

Hmmm, said Essie to herself. *I'm sure my toilet seat will be okay overnight. I'll just have to be extra careful when I sit on it and remember that Lorena broke it for me. I'll call Jake tomorrow. Right now, I have to finish my puzzle. A five-letter-word for overly romantic? Gushy? Sweet? Oh, I know. Mushy. Yes, that fits.*

With that, Essie was soon on a roll and her puzzle was quickly completed. *A successful day in more ways than one,* she told herself. *And a new toilet seat. Yes, it had been a very good day.* She hummed a snippet of that dance tune again. *What did they call it? Upside Funk?*

Chapter 3

The next morning, Essie was at her appointed table along with her three mates—Marjorie, Opal, and Fay—enjoying a delicious Happy Haven breakfast. Santos had just refilled their coffee cups. As soon as he left, Marjorie began to press Opal for information.

"So, Opal," she said coyly, "you must tell us all about this Lester Mills. Where did you meet him? He's really very attractive."

"I don't know him all that well, Marjorie," replied Opal, sipping her coffee. "He was a client of Mr. Brandt's—my boss. Actually, for a very long time. Mr. Brandt did Mr. Mills' business taxes and his personal taxes. He—I mean, Mr. Mills—was always very hands-on. He came to us himself, although I remember Mr. Brandt saying once that Mr. Mills' firm was so large that he probably could have, or should have, had in-house accountants. But, he'd been with our firm since he started his business, and he was very loyal."

"That's not something you see today," said Essie. "My John would have liked him. Most businessmen just go where they can get the best deal."

"True," agreed Opal, tugging on her pink opal necklace as she gazed off at the sunlight shining in through the floor-to-ceiling windows in the dining room. "But not Lester Mills. He was in our office every tax season just like clockwork. And as I said, not just his business taxes. His personal taxes too. And he always brought his wife along during tax season. They always came in holding hands. It was so sweet. They were so in love—even after many years of marriage." Opal again turned and gazed at dust motes floating in the sunbeams coming through the windows. Essie noted her strong profile and her long, aquiline nose.

"That's not something you see today much either," added Essie. "Old married couples are not usually so demonstrative in public."

"Speak for yourself, Essie," cried Marjorie. "I am a very passionate person and have no problem demonstrating my affection in public." She wiggled her fingertips around as if she were ready to grab the object of her affection.

"Yes, Marjorie," said Opal, taking a deep breath. "We have come to know that about you. How many husbands did you have again?"

"I had two, Opal; you know that—and maybe a boyfriend or two—before, between, and/or after the husbands, of course," she exclaimed demurely.

"Not *during*?" asked Essie, giving her friend a nudge.

"Essie!" cried the little redhead. "What do you take me for? Some kind of hussy?"

"Your word, Marjorie," said Essie. "Right, ladies?" She glanced at Opal. Fay giggled suddenly. All three of the women looked over at their wheelchair-bound friend, and Fay quickly picked up her coffee cup and stared at its contents. It was true that Marjorie was the most worldly of the group. Essie had been married to John, and they'd had three children. She was now a widow. Opal was a spinster. None of the women had any idea about Fay's love life—if she'd ever had a love life.

"Anyway," continued Opal, "if we are finished discussing Marjorie's extensive love life, I'd like to point out that Mr. Mills was always a gentleman when he had an appointment with Mr. Brandt. He was always courteous and polite to me, and when he brought his wife with him, his wife always remembered my name. I remember that after she died, he was still as thoughtful as before, but somehow he never seemed as energetic or lively as he'd been when she was alive. Even after many years." Opal became suddenly quiet and her face dropped.

"So, uh, when did his wife die?" asked Marjorie.

"Oh, many years ago," said Opal, looking up suddenly as if from a dream. "Let me see. I'd say maybe twenty years at least."

"Did he ever remarry?" queried Marjorie again.

"Oh, no," said Opal. "He was so devoted to her. He continued to be Mr. Brandt's client, of course, after she died. When I retired, he was still coming in for his tax reviews, so I saw him several times a year up until then. After that, I have no idea what he did."

"He seems very interested in you, Opal," said Marjorie.

"Oh, don't be silly," said Opal, blushing and waving her hand in a flustered manner.

"He asked you on a date."

"He just . . .mentioned sitting together to watch the fireworks display on the Fourth," Opal stammered.

"That's a date," said Marjorie, pointing her finger.

"It's not a date," replied Opal, shaking her head. "Is it, Essie? Essie, please take my side here."

"Why?" asked Essie. "I don't care if you hold hands with this guy on Independence Day. I don't care if you canoodle him in your apartment."

"Essie!" cried Opal. "Canoodle! How could you say such a thing?"

"What's wrong with canoodling? I thought it just meant hugging and kissing," sputtered Essie at her faux pas.

"I think it means more than that," whispered Opal.

"Oh, Opal," said Marjorie with a knowing look. "There's nothing wrong with you canoodling this Lester Mills if you want to—or even more than canoodling. But, please, if you decide against canoodling him, give me first dibs at him." She raised her eyebrows up and down. "I'll canoodle his pants off."

"You're welcome to him," replied Opal. "I'm not romantically interested in him. He's just an acquaintance."

"So that's why you blush every time we mention his name?" asked Essie.

"I do not!" declared Opal, blushing profusely.

"I rest my case," said Essie, pointing her finger at Opal's increasingly red face.

"I can't help it. It's a neurological reaction. It has nothing to do with Lester—I mean Mr. Mills."

"Oh, it's Lester now," teased Marjorie.

"Will you two stop it?" pleaded Opal.

"I'm sorry, Opal," said Essie.

"I'm not," said Marjorie. "Opal is always so prim and proper. It's fun to see her outside her comfort zone and all girly-girly over some man."

"Oh, it's that horrible dance," admitted Opal, almost panting.

"What?" asked Essie. "You mean, the upside down funky? Or whatever?"

"Yes, that thing," cried Opal. "Now I can't even think of Lester—I mean Mr. Mills—without seeing him up there gyrating his hips about like some low-life Hollywood stripper."

"And what's so bad about that?" asked Marjorie.

"It's just not the image I always had of him. He was always such a sweet, gentle man. So soft-spoken and considerate. Seeing him dance like that, well, it just doesn't fit with the image I had of him."

"Really, Opal," argued Marjorie, "if the poor man can't break out and have a little fun now, at his age, when can he? I mean, we're in a retirement home. When *will* the time be right for all of us? Any of us? To break out of the image that people have of us? If not now, when?"

"I agree with Marjorie on this, Opal," said Essie. "I'm sure your Mr. Mills is a lovely gentleman; you mustn't judge him too harshly. He has no one to report to now. What's wrong with him letting his hair down a little? He certainly appeared to be having a good time while he was dancing. You said that after his wife died he seemed to lose interest in life. Well, it seems that dancing may have given him that interest back. Or maybe it was seeing *you* that has given him that interest back."

"I don't know . . . ." Opal sighed, now clutching her necklace with both hands.

"Come on, Opal," urged Marjorie, "give him a chance. If he wants to sit with you at the fireworks display, what harm can it do? You two can reminisce and enjoy the evening. Is that so bad?"

"I . . . I'll think about it," replied the tall woman, now looking down at her necklace and chewing on her lip.

"Hello, ladies!" announced a friendly voice. The threesome looked up from their spirited discussion to see an attractive man with lush, dark curly hair, tanned skin, and large deep brown eyes.

"Oh, Felix!" said Marjorie.

"Greetings, to my favorite table!" said Felix Federico, manager of Happy Haven. All four ladies smiled with joy. Their new manager was such a marked improvement over their previous one—a very sour old woman who was much more concerned with saving money than pleasing the residents. Felix Federico had made it his duty to get to know each and every resident at Happy Haven personally and he was certainly one of the most gregarious and cheerful people Essie had ever met. She had no idea if he was actually running Happy Haven efficiently, but his rapport with the residents was top notch.

"Mr. Federico," began Opal.

"Felix," corrected the manager. "Miss Opal, you know you can call me Felix." When he said this, he took Opal's hand and looked deeply into her eyes. Essie could see Opal melt a bit inside. She wasn't actually certain if Felix Federico's behavior was within the bounds of good managerial techniques or if it entered the territory of flirting, but she quickly dismissed this thought, because she too enjoyed the manager's attentions and she knew he would eventually bestow his charm on her.

"Felix," Opal corrected herself, noticeably shaking as she extricated her hand from his. "Um, Felix, we were talking about the upcoming fireworks display."

"Oh, si," he replied. "I love this country! We celebrate its birth with the shooting of the fireworks. How amazing! How deliriously wonderful! Yes, I hope you all will enjoy this magnificent event and come out on the front lawn on the Fourth day of July. We will set up chairs and a nice picnic buffet. Isn't it remarkable that the city of Reardon has this amazing fireworks display in their city park and that the city park is so close to Happy Haven that we can all stay right here and see it right from our front lawn?" Essie knew that their new manager was a native of some Latin country but she wasn't certain which.

"It is amazing, Felix." Marjorie. She fluttered her eyelashes at him.

"Ah, Miss Marjorie," he said to her, moving around the table and grabbing her hand. "How is my favorite redhead today?"

"Oh, Felix," Marjorie giggled, eyes still fluttering. "You're such a tease."

"Oh, and there's my sweet, shy, little quiet girl," he said, moving on to Fay in her wheelchair. Fay looked up at the tall man, straining her neck to do so as he was standing extremely close to her. "How are you today, Fay?" Fay just smiled. Felix squatted down beside the wheelchair and took Fay's hand. He bent near her so that his mouth was quite close to her ear and talked very softly. Essie was unable to hear what he was saying, but it was clear from the fact that his lips were moving and the fact that Fay was reacting noticeably that he was speaking to her.

"Oh, Felix," said Marjorie, as Felix's conversation with Fay continued on, "Fay doesn't really respond to anything you say, you know." Felix ignored Marjorie's comment and continued to speak quietly to Fay. The other women glanced at each other, uncertain whether they should speak out loud or ignore the intimate conversation that was taking place between Fay and the manager. After a while, Felix stood up, bent over, and kissed Fay's hand. Then he turned to the table and gave a polite bow.

"Have a lovely day, ladies," he said, and with that, he was on his way to another table.

"My goodness," whispered Marjorie, after he'd left. "That was a very intimate, very long conversation he had with Fay."

"Oh, twaddle waddle, Marjorie," replied Essie. "You're just jealous that he spent more time with Fay than with you."

"At least I can speak back to him," said Marjorie.

"Marjorie!" cried Opal. "That's mean."

They all looked over at Fay, who seemed to be totally ignoring them, her eyes focused on the glittering chandelier in the center of the dining room.

"You can't have every man at Happy Haven, after all," added Opal.

"Me?" cried Marjorie. "I don't have *any* man at Happy Haven. It seems like you have someone, Opal, and now Fay has Felix. Probably Essie will start dating the UPS man and where will that put me?" She stuck out her lower lip and pouted sweetly.

"It will put you where we all are. Single. Just like we were yesterday and the day before. I am perfectly happy with that condition. I came in here single and am happy to remain that way." Essie reflected Marjorie's pout with a determined grimace. "Now, ladies," she cried. "We sound like a bunch of teenage girls fighting over the local football quarterback. We are mature women. We don't fight over men."

"Maybe you don't, Essie," declared Marjorie, "but I do when I see my fellow tablemates snapping up all the eligible ones."

"No one is snapping up anybody," said Opal.

"Oh, really?" asked Marjorie, pointing at Fay, who ignored them all as she happily stared off, a giant smile on her chubby round face.

Chapter 4

After breakfast and an extra lengthy second cup of coffee, Essie finally left the dining room and casually rolled her walker through the lobby back to her apartment. She waved at Happy Haven's main receptionist Phyllis at the front desk and smiled at several other residents who were seated around the lobby in some of the comfy sofas and arm chairs. She looked at the far end of the lobby to a group of people waiting for the elevator. The group included Opal's old friend and new Happy Haven resident, Lester Mills, and two young men and a young woman. They all appeared to be together, as they were talking in a quiet but rather animated fashion. Essie, being the curious soul that she was, slowed her progression through the lobby, so she could hopefully hear what Opal's new heartthrob was saying to these young people.

"Come on, Dad," said the taller of the two young men. "It'll only take a half hour or so."

"Yeah," agreed the other male. "We can have you back here in time for lunch—if you really want to eat here." He made a face.

"Oh, I don't know," said Lester, reluctantly, with a strained smile. "I'm really happy with things the way they are . . ."

"What can you be happy about?" demanded the young woman, in a controlled whisper. "You're letting the company go under, Dad. Surely, you don't want that?"

The elevator door opened, the four of them entered, and the door closed. Essie continued on to her apartment, wondering what that little snippet of conversation had been about. It appeared that the young people with Lester were his children and they were attempting to convince him of something business-related and Lester was reluctant to go along with their demand. Curious. Maybe Opal would know what it was all about. Essie would ask her at lunch.

Essie arrived at her apartment and again her bare door struck her forcefully with its emptiness. She really needed to get going on her decoration. Other residents were already festooning their doors with holiday bows and ribbons. Essie knew what she was going to do, and it was time to put her plan into action before the Fourth arrived and it was too late. She opened her door and scooted her walker quickly inside. Sitting in her rocker, she quickly placed a phone call to the main office.

"Oh, hello, this is Essie Cobb in 3B. I need Handyman Jake to come and fix my toilet immediately." The woman in the office said she would send Jake right down. *That's good*, thought Essie. *There's nothing like a toilet emergency to get this place hopping.*

"Attention, residents!" called out the loud speaker in Essie's living room as Phyllis's voice began the morning announcements. "Don't forget, everyone! It's not long before our big Fourth of July celebration. Get your door decorated and plan your costume. We expect all residents to be outfitted in red, white, and blue costumes on the Fourth. There will be prizes for the best door decoration and the best costume. We'll even have a photographer here from the local paper, so everyone, let's really give it our all!"

Oh, I'll give it my all, thought Essie. *Just you wait till you see my door.*

She picked up her telephone and dialed again.

"Oh, hello, Ned," she said when the phone was answered almost immediately. "It's your grandma Essie."

"Grandma!" replied her grandson, cheerfully. "How goes it? How's the new answering machine? No more problems, I hope?"

"No, no," said Essie, "It's fine. But I do have another problem I'd like your technical help with, if you have the time."

"For you, Grandma, I will make time," said the young man.

"Great! Well, I don't even know if you can do what I want, but I thought if anyone could, it would be my Ned." Essie poured on the compliments.

"Grandma, is that you using flattery to get me to help you?" He chuckled. "You don't need to do that. I'd love to help you out. What do you need?"

Essie began to explain her technical requirements. She spoke for a long time and gave Ned a very elaborate explanation. When she'd finished, she heaved a big sigh and said, "Oh, Ned, I'm afraid all of this is just too much to ask."

"Oh, no, Grandma. I think I know exactly what you want and I think I can do it for you quite easily. How about I drop by and we'll whip it up?"

"Drop by? Whip it up?"

"Yeah," he replied. "I'm heading to work now. You're on my way. I'll just stop by your place and we'll get this project done in a flash, okay?"

"A flash?" asked Essie, skeptically. She envisioned the so-called "flash mob" from the men's dance the previous evening.

"Yep," said Ned. "I promise."

"Okay," she replied, cautiously, "if you really think we can do it . . ."

"Oh, I *know* we can do it," said Ned. "I'll be there in just a bit. Bye." And with that, he hung up.

Essie was flummoxed by the speed with which Ned had understood her plan and figured out how to help her. She had assumed what she wanted to be a very complex undertaking, but . . .well, maybe with Ned's technological skills . . . it would be easier than she'd envisioned.

There was a knock on the door.

"Miss Essie, it's Jake."

"Oh, just a minute," she replied, rising and scooting her walker to the doorway and opening it. Jake, the Happy Haven handyman stood there. He was a large, rotund man with a crew cut and a reddish smiling face. His tool belt hung way below his waist which bulged over the top like a cake bubbling out of a pan in the oven. He was leaning jauntily against the door frame, carrying a tool box in his free hand.

"Your toilet's overflowing?"

"Oh, well, no," said Essie, somewhat embarrassed. "It's actually broken, but not overflowing. Can you come take a look?"

"'Course, ma'am," he replied as he lumbered down Essie's hallway to the bathroom. Essie rushed behind him as fast as she could roll her walker, trying to intervene before he arrived at her toilet. She scooted in between Jake and the toilet and reached down and pulled up the lid. Then with dramatic gestures and facial expressions, she said, "You see, the seat is very loose! I almost fall in when I sit on it. Why, this morning, I slid right onto the floor when I tried to sit down!" She grabbed the seat and shook it vigorously back and forth. The damage Lorena had caused the previous night had definitely ruined the seat, and it clung to life just barely by one screw on one end.

"Yup," said Jake, plopping his tool box on the floor. "I'd say I'd just reattach it, Miss Essie, but the wood in the seat is broken too. Look. You can see where it's splintered. I'm going to have to get you a new seat altogether."

"Oh, no!" cried Essie, drawing her face into a fake frown. It was all she could do to keep from smiling.

"Oh, it's nothing, ma'am," said Jake. "A new toilet seat ain't expensive. Think we got a few extras down in the supply room. Here. Just let me remove this damaged one and I'll take it out and dispose of it and bring you back a new one."

"No!" cried Essie.

"No?" asked Jake, taken aback.

"I mean, yes, I want a new seat, but please don't throw the old one out, Jake. Just leave it here with me and I'll dispose of it in my trash." She chuckled self-consciously.

"Oh, Miss Essie, it's too big and clunky to squeeze into your trash can. Just let me take it to the garbage bin out back. It's no trouble at all."

"Please, Jake! I really want to . . . uh . . . keep it . . . for sentimental reasons." She smiled sweetly.

"You have a sentimental attachment to your toilet seat?"

"Uh, yes. I've had it for a long time and I've grown fond of it."

Jake scowled and looked at her strangely.

"Okay, if that's what you want, but it's no trouble."

"Just take it off and get me a new one, Jake. I'll deal with this old one."

"If you say so, Miss Essie," said the handyman. He quickly made short work of the defective seat using a wrench and screwdriver, and then headed out her door. Essie stood there after she'd closed the door, clutching the old toilet seat to her chest triumphantly.

She'd barely said good-by to Jake when there was another knock on the door.

"Grandma! It's Ned!"

"Ned!" Essie exclaimed. She hung onto the toilet seat with one hand as she reached over her walker and opened the door. "That was quick."

"A toilet seat, Grandma?" Ned asked, looking down at the large circular object smashed against her chest. "Is this part of your plan?"

"Actually, yes, it is," she announced, ushering him in quickly and shutting the door behind him.

"Well, let's get busy then. I have to get to work."

Essie explained her plan for her door decoration to her grandson.

"Now, let me see if I have this right," Ned reiterated. "You in the outfit we discussed, to fit inside, right?"

"Right," she said.

"I'll have to measure it all," said Ned and he pulled a wind-up tape measure from his pocket. He checked the dimensions of the toilet seat.

"Do you need some paper to write that all down?" asked Essie, heading for her desk.

"Oh, no, Grandma," replied Ned. "I'll just jot it down in my iPhone notes." He pulled out his smart phone, pressed some buttons and entered the information. "Now, about that photograph."

"Oh, yes," she said. "Where's your camera?" She looked around.

"Right here, Grandma," he said, showing her his cellphone.

"You can take my picture with your telephone?"

"Yes. And a lot more. You just wait and see what I can do with this phone."

"Oh, Ned, I don't have my costume ready. I have some parts of it ready in my bedroom, but . . ."

"Tell me again, what you're dressing up to be . . ." Ned prompted.

Essie regaled him with a description of the outfit she'd planned to wear as her holiday costume. From the elaborate head-gear all the way down to the shoes, she gave a very detailed description. Ned asked questions and Essie responded in a way that indicated she was going for an exact historical recreation.

"I think I've got it, Grandma," said Ned. "I can create all that with Photoshop."

"Photo who?" asked Essie.

"It's a digital program that allows me to take your picture and then make you look different, or as if you're wearing a costume *after* I take the picture."

"You can do that?"

"I can. I can change it in any way I want and I can make it any size or shape I want. So I'll be certain it fits your needs and our specifications exactly."

"Wonderful!"

"Okay, now, Grandma, give me your best Fourth of July smile so I can get a good shot." He held up his camera and Essie grinned. He took a few snaps from different angles and distances and then pressed another button so he could show Essie what they looked like.

"Fred's beds!" she gasped. "I can't believe you did that so fast and got so many great pictures."

"Well, I had a great model," he said, warmly. "I need to get going now, Grandma, but I'll be back later with the finished product. Don't worry."

"Thank you, Ned," she said, walking him to the door. "You're so wonderful." The young man headed out just as Jake the handyman was arriving back with a new toilet seat. The two men nodded at each other as Jake came in, showing Essie the brand new, shiny seat.

She followed Jake back to the bathroom where he installed the new seat in a few minutes and then asked her to test it.

"I'm not going to sit on a toilet seat in front of a man, Jake," Essie cried, indignantly.

"Suit yourself," replied Jake, giving the seat a final shake to make certain it was firmly attached. Then he grabbed his toolkit and departed, mumbling something that sounded to Essie a lot like *women*.

Chapter 5

Soon after, Essie was alone in the art room. She was happy that none of the other residents were around to see her working on her door decoration. Also, she didn't want to have to answer all sorts of embarrassing questions about what she was doing there with a toilet seat. The art room featured several long tables with shelves along the walls filled with art supplies. Essie had set her toilet seat on a table and was presently wrapping it in patriotic crepe paper—red, white and blue. When she finished wrapping the seat, she secreted it back in her walker's basket. Then she moseyed around the art room looking for additional supplies she might use to put the finishing touches on her costume, which was only partially done and hanging at the back of her closet. She selected several units of Styrofoam, glue, wire, wire cutters, heavy string, green shiny wrapping paper, a Styrofoam wreath, and gold glitter. Dumping everything on top of her newly decorated toilet seat in the basket of her walker, and covering it all with her sweater, she headed back down to her apartment.

Getting on the elevator to return to the first floor, she was followed inside the compartment by the three young adults she'd seen earlier with Opal's new friend Lester Mills. They all smiled at her politely but none of them said a word. Essie smiled and greeted them.

"Lovely weather we're having, isn't it?" she threw out, thinking that was absolutely not the way to extract information about the new Mr. Mills. Her sleuthing skills were failing her.

The Mills children mumbled their greetings but otherwise kept quiet. When they all got off the elevator, the three young people stormed off and headed out of Happy Haven. Essie noted that they all seemed annoyed and highly motivated. They didn't appear to have just come from a friendly visit to their aged father. She determined to discuss the situation with Opal more when she saw her later.

Back in her apartment, Essie removed all of her supplies for her costume from her walker basket and placed them on her bed. She then went into her walk-in closet and retrieved a large green blanket that was draped over a hanger in the very back. She brought it out and, twisting the top of the wire hanger, hung the blanket at the top of the bedroom door. She also went back into her closet and used her step stool to climb up and reach onto a high shelf where she brought down a small round hatbox. Placing it on her bed, she opened it to reveal a small beige cloche hat. She set the hat on her head. It fit perfectly, just like a little cap. Removing the hat, she studied it and glanced at the supplies and tools on her bed.

Quickly, Essie used her tools and supplies to create her Fourth of July costume. She decorated the Styrofoam wreath in the green wrapping paper and attached it to the cloche hat. She wrapped eight small pointed cylinders in green paper and glued them to the outside of the wreath. She wrapped a large Styrofoam cylinder in the green wrapping paper, and put gold sequins all over a Styrofoam ball and attached the ball to the end of the cylinder. She found a large, old book in the bookshelf in her living room and wrapped that in green paper too. When she was all done putting the pieces together, she decided to try on her costume. Removing the green blanket from the hanger, she wrapped herself in it like an old Roman toga. She placed the hat with the green wreath and green spikes on her head and then she picked up the green book in one hand and the gold-sequined-topped green cylinder in the other. She stood in front of her dresser mirror to see the final result.

Oh, my! she thought. *I look just like the real thing.*

There was a knock on the door. Essie lifted the folds of the green blanket, partially draping them over her walker and shuffled over to her door.

"It's me, Grandma," announced Ned as Essie opened the door. But it was Ned who was surprised when he saw Essie in her costume. "Wow! Grandma, that's quite a costume. You look great! 'Give me your tired, your poor.'" He was holding a long cardboard tube.

"And it's not red, white, and blue," said Essie with great satisfaction. "Everybody around here thinks that patriotic means red, white, and blue." She escorted her grandson into her apartment and closed the door, following him into the living room where he sat on the couch and she carefully situated her robe before sliding into her rocker.

"I mean, really, Grandma. You did a great job. I hope you'll like what I did too." He removed the lid from the tube and slid out a roll of heavy paper. When he unrolled it, the shape was a perfect small oval—just the exact size of Essie's toilet seat. He held it up for Essie to see.

"Oh, crimy blimy!" shouted Essie. "It's me! How did you do that, Ned?" For indeed, the photograph showed Essie's head almost as it appeared now with her green hat with the spiked green wreath. And even more, her entire face and hair were green.

"I told you, Grandma," he said, "it's called Photoshop. I took those photographs of you this morning, then I used this program. Look!" He pulled out his cellphone and tapped on a small square which immediately opened up into a special program. "See. Here's the photograph of your face. Well, first I edited it a bit and cleaned it up, then I changed the color a bit and just added the decorations I wanted to make you look like . . . well, like you do now."

"It's amazing, Ned!" said Essie. "And it looks like it will fit perfectly in the toilet seat."

"Oh, it will," he replied. "I measured it. Remember. Then when I got just the look I wanted, I took it over to a local print shop and had then run it off on some heavier paper so it would hold up when we attached it to the seat."

"Ned, you think of everything!" cried Essie. "I'm sure I'll win the door decoration contest now."

"And the costume contest too," added Ned.

"You think so?" Essie asked.

"How could you not? Just look at that face!" cried Ned. He pointed at Essie's face on the roll of paper. "Now that's a patriotic face if I ever saw one."

"Yes!" exclaimed Essie, "that crazy green face!"

"Now, let's get busy. Get me that toilet seat and . . ."

"I've got glue," announced Essie.

"I've got better," he said, pulling a staple gun from his jacket pocket. "This will hold your photo to that toilet seat." Essie leaped up as best as she could leap up and rolled speedily into her bedroom and quickly returned with the decorated toilet seat.

"Wow! That's a beauty! Almost hate to touch it, it's so spectacular," said Ned taking the red, white, and blue toilet seat from Essie. He placed it on Essie's coffee table, turned it over, and carefully centered the photo of Essie face down on the opening in the seat. Then, using his staple gun, he quickly snapped it in place all around the edge of the picture. When he was finished, he turned the seat over and held it up for the two of them to see. Truly, the toilet seat, with a costumed Essie in the middle was a most original, if not *the* most original door decoration Happy Haven had probably ever seen.

"It's perfect!" she cried. "Now, let's hang it on the door."

"I'm ready for that too," answered Ned, pulling out some picture hanging nails and a hammer. With a few pounds, he attached a clip to the back of the seat and strode over to hang it from the nail that was already on Essie's door. Then both grandmother and grandson stood and admired their handiwork for a while before returning back inside and sitting down in Essie's living room.

"That is so impressive, Ned," said Essie. "And you say I could do that photo shopping thing on the computer here at Happy Haven?"

"Absolutely, Grandma, you could, but even better, you could just use a smart phone like I have, then you could do it all right here in your apartment."

"Oh, I don't know . . ." said Essie, with a sigh. "I really like the Happy Haven computer. It took me a long time to figure it out. I'd hate to have to figure out something else. That phone of yours has so many buttons and knobs . . ."

"Not all that many, Grandma. Besides, you're the smartest grandma I know. You'd catch on really fast, I'm sure."

"I doubt that." She shrugged.

"You know, Grandma, having your own smart phone would save you time. You wouldn't have to always run down to the computer room every time you wanted to find out something or do some research for one of your cases." Ned had helped Essie investigate a number of mysteries that had occurred at Happy Haven over the years.

"I do spend a lot of time there," she agreed, nodding.

"And all that pressure you get from Mom and Aunt Pru about not being here to answer your landline phone would end. You can take your smart phone with you so you can answer it anywhere you go."

"Now that's a reason I *don't* like," said Essie, defiantly. "I like to be able to get away from the telephone from time to time."

"Strange," said Ned, contemplating. "I don't know anyone who feels that way. Most everyone I know can't bear to be separated from their phone."

"Maybe that's what's wrong with them," declared Essie, giving her grandson a knowing look.

"Well, you may have something there, Grandma," he agreed. "You do know how to relax and enjoy your life. I like that about you."

"And well you should," Essie added. "You young people are just go, go, go. You need to stop and smell the roses sometimes."

"You're right," he said, "but if I was out smelling roses right now, Grandma, you wouldn't have your door decoration done, now would you?"

"Touché," she replied. "I don't think you've quite convinced me to get a smart phone . . ."

"You know, Grandma," said Ned, surreptitiously, "Nothing would stir up Mom and Aunt Pru more than if you started using a smart phone and became all phone savvy. They both think they're smarter than you because they're so good with their phones, but *I* could teach you stuff that would blow their minds, that would make you far more technologically advanced than both of them."

"You could?" she asked, perking up—the idea of besting her two daughters in such a way appealing to her.

"Ah ha! I should have started with that. Pull one over on your daughters. You are a devil, Grandma.

Listen, how about after the Fourth and all of your decorating and costuming is done and things have settled down, we get together and I show you all the fabulous things you can do with a smart phone—things that your daughters don't know anything about?"

"Hmm," she mused. "I do like the sound of that, Ned." She nodded. "I do like the sound of that."

Chapter 6

The Fourth of July finally arrived. By this time, residents at Happy Haven had all decorated their apartment doors. Most doors were festooned with American flags and crepe paper streamers. Only Essie Cobb's door featured a red, white, and blue toilet seat with the face of Essie as the Statue of Liberty peeking out from inside at potential visitors. Essie realized, as she careened around Happy Haven to view all the doors, that hers was certainly the most unique. *I'm was sure to win the prize,* she concluded.

Some of the residents were already in their costumes first thing in the morning, but Essie had decided to save her "big reveal" until suppertime. Until then, she just wore her blue trousers and a red shirt.

Right before supper, Essie flung her large green blanket around her body and donned her new green hat that she'd built with Ned's help. She placed the green torch and green book in the basket of her walker and headed off to the dining room. As she rolled through the lobby, she could feel all eyes on her as residents immediately realized who (or rather *what*) she was supposed to be. When she arrived at her table, Marjorie, Opal and Fay were already seated.

"Give me your tired, your poor!" declared Essie, turning around slowly for the entire room to see her, lifting the green torch and the green book into the appropriate Statue of Liberty pose. The dining hall erupted in applause and Essie turned out to the full group and gave a small bow.

"Go, Essie!" cried one man from a corner table, and all the residents laughed.

"You mean, Lady Liberty!" Essie responded. She replaced her two props back into her basket and, gathering her green blanket robe up, slid into her chair.

"Essie," said Marjorie when Essie had turned back to her tablemates, "that is a marvelous get-up."

"Thank you, Marjorie. I had a lot of help from my grandson."

"I saw your door decoration too," added Opal. "You put a lot of work into that."

"Yes," replied Essie. "I don't just sit around letting things *go to pot*." Essie snickered.

"No, Essie, it's not like you to let things get *flushed* away!" added Marjorie.

"Creating it must have been very tiring," said Opal, "I bet when you finished it, you were really *pooped.*"

The women cackled so much at their own cleverness that they soon gathered some looks from nearby tables.

"Anyway, you're sure to win best costume *and* best door," announced Marjorie.

"Well, thank you," said Essie, sweetly, "but you all look wonderful too." She glanced around at her three friends. They were all dressed in sparkly, patriotic finery. Opal was wearing a full-length, long-sleeved red gown with a blue and white sash at the waist. Marjorie had on a cocktail-length dress in sparkly blue sequins and her hair was done up on top of her head with a jeweled tiara, and even Fay was dressed all in white—a white top and white slacks with white sneakers and a red baseball cap.

"I helped Fay," said Opal as Essie's eyes fell on their silent friend, "pick out an outfit from her closet."

"You look adorable, Fay," said Marjorie. Fay responded with a beaming smile.

"Essie," said Opal, "you really stand out because you're all in green. Everyone else is red, white and blue."

"I know," replied Essie. "Not so dumb, eh?"

The four of them laughed, and soon they were sipping the last of their iced tea.

"So, Opal," began Marjorie, "any more plans regarding meeting your new beau Lester to watch the fireworks later tonight?"

"Oh, I don't know, Marjorie," said Opal, hesitatingly, "I'm sure he was just being polite . . ."

"It won't hurt to find out," suggested Essie. "You look like you're all dolled up for a date. We'd hate to see that outfit go to waste . . ." And, indeed, Essie had never seen quite so much of Opal's cleavage in all the years she'd known her at Happy Haven.

"I'll see," offered Opal, starting to rise. "If he's there, he's there. If he sits next to me, I can't stop him, now, can I?"

"Opal, you're such a romantic," said Marjorie, as all four women left the table and headed out of the dining room.

Several hours later, after darkness had fallen, residents began to gather on the front lawn of Happy Haven. Management had arranged groupings of lawn chairs around, facing east where the city of Reardon's city park was located, just a few blocks down the street. Under the canopy over the front entrance, a table displaying appropriate treats had been set up. There were boxes of crackerjacks and pitchers of lemonade with paper cups. Some residents were still in their costumes and some (mostly those who had worn more elaborate wear) had changed into more comfortable outfits.

Essie left her room around eight, figuring that would give her plenty of time to mill around and chat with people before the actual fireworks began. She had changed out of her Lady Liberty costume into her more comfortable outfit of blue slacks, red top, and sneakers. She also wore a white sweater just in case it got chilly after dark. She exited the front entrance, saying hello to Phyllis at the front desk, and meandered over to the refreshment table where she nibbled on some crackerjacks. Felix Federico was manning the refreshment counter and he poured Essie a glass of lemonade.

"Miss Essie," he said sweetly. "Or should I say, Lady Liberty? That was a fabulous costume! Would you care for some lemonade?"

"Thank you, Felix.," She blushed.

She wandered around the front yard of Happy Haven, speaking to various residents along the way. Many of the people she saw, she hadn't seen in a long time as many residents ate at a different time than she did or lived in a different hallway or even on the second floor. *My*, she thought, *Happy Haven is really getting big!*

She saw Marjorie sitting with a group of women she knew and sauntered over to them.

"Essie Cobb!" said one. "Where's your Statue of Liberty costume? That was the best costume I've ever seen at Happy Haven!"

"Thank you, Maude," replied Essie, glad she remembered the woman's name and wondering how Maude had remembered hers. Remembering peoples' names was a constant struggle for Essie and, she assumed, for many of the other residents too. "It was a little hard to maneuver in, and I was afraid I might trip over the blanket out here in the dark."

"Oh, of course," replied Maude. Essie had no idea what her last name was.

"Where are Opal and Fay?" Essie asked Marjorie.

"Oh, they're here somewhere," replied Marjorie, waving her hand around.

"Did Opal ever locate that . . um, you know," whispered Essie.

"Oh, you mean Lester," said Marjorie out loud. "I don't know. I started talking with these ladies here and I got all caught up. Go look for her, Essie." She gave Essie a swat on her behind and giggled.

Essie wondered what Marjorie had put in her lemonade which she was now guzzling down with abandon. The lemonade *Essie* was drinking was certainly non-alcoholic. Oh, it was probably just Marjorie's out-going personality. It usually was.

Essie skimmed over the moist grass, pushing her walker with more difficulty than usual, weaving in and out among the lawn chairs, greeting various residents along the way. It was getting darker now and the further out from the building Essie went, the harder it was to see anything. Even so, she kept moving. Finally, far out, almost to the street, in the distance, she could see a grouping of lawn chairs with two people seated and a third person in a wheel chair next to them. She stared for a while until she was certain that she was looking at Opal, with her "gentleman caller" Lester on one side, and Fay in her wheel chair on the other side. Opal always took Fay with her wherever she went. Essie mused as to how that practice would work if Opal and Lester decided to actually "date." Opal and Lester were chatting softly and Fay was looking around with awe. This was obviously not the type of adventure that Fay got to take very often.

Essie hesitated, not certain if she should interrupt this potentially romantic interlude. However, as she was contemplating her next move, Lester looked up and glanced over to where Essie was standing. Seeing her standing alone, he called out to her.

"Essie!" he cried, waving at her. "Opal, there's your friend," he remarked to Opal, turning to her.

"Essie!" yelled Opal, also waving for her to join them.

Essie guided her walker with difficulty through the moist grass, which was decidedly thicker this much further from the building, until she was standing in front of the threesome. Fay smiled and bounced a little when she saw Essie.

"Essie, come join us," said Opal. "We have wonderful seats for the fireworks."

"Yes," agreed Lester. "They've started already. Look!" He pointed towards the east, "You can see over those rooftops. That's where the city park is." And in truth, Essie glanced sideways to see a glorious display of sparkling lights fill the night sky.

"Well, I would," hesitated Essie, "but I don't see any extra lawn chairs around here." She searched around but all nearby chairs appeared to be occupied.

"No matter," said Lester. "You can take my chair and I'll go find another one." Another burst of light shattered the air and all of the Happy Haven residents ooed and awed.

"Oh, no!" exclaimed Essie, fearful now of ruining Opal's "almost" date. "I don't want to intrude. I'll just go sit with some other people I know." She started to turn her walker around. But it was too late. Lester was already pushing himself out of his flimsy lawn chair, and having some difficulty doing so. As he pushed on the arm rests, they almost gave way.

"Wait, Essie!" he called. "Don't go! Here!" He finally succeeded in rising and standing. He moved over to Essie and touched her arm, pointing out his chair and offering to help her sit. Essie sighed and gave Opal an "I'm sorry" facial expression. The last thing she'd intended was to spoil Opal's "date." "Bang, bang, bang!" she heard as a giant flower-like display rose to great height in the sky and then each bud opened separately—one after the other, like a blooming flower of fire. Lester carefully guided Essie back to his chair, and as she turned around to lower herself into the seat, Lester moved her walker to the side of the chair so that it would be there for her. "There you go, young lady," said Lester as he tapped the arm-rests to be certain that Essie was firmly and safely seated. "I'm going to go find myself another chair. You and Opal—and Fay—can chat while I'm gone." He gave all three women a big smile. Essie glanced over at Opal and Fay, and they all smiled at each other and then at Lester who was still bending protectively over Essie.

Lester looked up over Essie's head at the sky to the west and suddenly his face changed from a polite gentlemanly smile to one of terror. With no warning or explanation, he suddenly leaped forward on top of Essie, knocking her and her chair over backwards and to the left, away from Opal and Fay—just before a firecracker came hurtling down, crashing right into Lester's bottom.

Opal screamed, and suddenly there was pandemonium on the front lawn of Happy Haven.

Chapter 7

When Essie opened her eyes, she found herself staring into the face of a young man.

"Ma'am?" he said to her. "Can you hear me?" He pressed a stethoscope to Essie's chest and attempted to listen to her heartbeat.

"Stop that!" Essie cried, pushing the man back so that she could sit up. She found herself sprawled on the grass. Looking around, she noticed chaos. There were ambulances, police cars, and lots of noise. Many Happy Haven residents were standing around her, all looking worried. "What happened?"

Opal appeared to Essie's left. "Oh, Essie, are you all right?"

"Of course I'm all right, Opal."

"She doesn't seem to have lost any memory function," said the young EMT hovering over Essie to his female colleague, who was kneeling on the ground on the other side of Essie.

"Just take it easy, ma'am," said the young woman. "You're going to be fine."

"Of course, I'm going to be fine," repeated Essie. "Will someone please tell me what happened. Why am I lying on the grass?"

"Oh, Essie," cried Opal. "You were firecrackered! It was just horrifying!"

"What? What do you mean I was firecrackered?" asked Essie. "What was horrifying, Opal? One minute I'm watching the fireworks display and the next minute I'm flat on my back." The EMTs were now checking

Essie's vital signs with blood pressure cuffs and ear thermometers.

"Looks like you got quite a bruise on the back of your head when you fell, ma'am," said the male EMT. "You were out for a bit . . ."

"Out?"

"Yes, ma'am," he said. "Unconscious." The two EMTs continued their testing and attempts to make Essie comfortable. "We'll be moving you in just a bit, ma'am. We just want to be certain you have no broken bones before we move you."

"There's nothing broken," declared Essie, attempting to stand, which resulted in her becoming suddenly dizzy and plopping back down on the ground.

"Now, ma'am," said the young woman, "please, just take it easy. We'd rather you just remain here and stay calm until they decide whether to take you to the hospital or not . . ."

"No hospital!" cried Essie. "I'm fine. I'm just a little dizzy." Her head throbbed at bit in back, but other than that, she felt okay.

"Essie, behave," whispered Opal, now kneeling beside her friend. Essie huffed but followed Opal's orders.

"Opal, bluebells from hell! What happened?"

"Lester saved your life, Essie."

"What?"

"He saved you. If he hadn't leaped on top of you and knocked your chair over, that firecracker would have struck you in the back of your head."

"What are you talking about?" asked Essie, now totally confused.

"You didn't see it. It came from behind you, but Lester must have looked up just as it was coming down, and he leaped on top of you and over you both went, chair and all. The firecracker hit him instead." Opal retold the tale with intensity but Essie noted that tears fell from her eyes as she recounted how the firecracker had hit Lester. "In his . . . um, rear end, Essie."

"Your friend is right, ma'am," said the EMT who was examining Essie's eyes now with a small light. "It could have been much worse if that firecracker had hit you directly. As it was, you just appear to have received a small superficial bruise on your head."

"Oh, my," said Essie, the extent of the event suddenly hitting her. "Was I . . . uh, unconscious . . . for long?"

"I don't know, ma'am," said the female. "We just got here."

"Not long, Essie," said Opal. "I think no more than a few minutes. The ambulance got here really fast. We're so lucky the hospital is just down the street. They dealt with Lester first." Her voice caught and she checked a sob. "They took him to the hospital already. Then they started to help you."

"So Lester saved my life?" Essie asked, still not totally certain what had just transpired.

"Yes, Essie; he must have looked up towards the west just as that firecracker was coming in and saw it and made a split second decision to leap on top of you to save you. If he hadn't . . ." Her voice trailed off and her eyes met Essie's eyes. The two women just looked at each other and knew that Essie had survived a life-threatening incident.

"And you say Lester was injured, Opal?" asked Essie.

Opal dabbed her eyes with her hanky as she said, "Yes, he was hit by the firecracker. In his . . . behind. He was unconscious when they took him away in the ambulance. Oh, Essie!" The tear drops suddenly turned into a torrent of tears. Just then, Marjorie arrived, pushing and shoving her way between policemen, EMTs and many residents.

"Essie! Opal! Are you okay? Where's Fay?"

"We're all fine, Marjorie. Fay's right over there," replied Opal, pointing a short distance where Fay was seated in her wheelchair, surrounded by several other residents, and following the action with great interest.

"What happened? People are saying Essie got hit by a firecracker!"

"They're wrong," snorted Essie, still seated on the ground. The EMTs had moved to one side and were now apparently conferring by radio with doctors back at the hospital, or at least that was what it appeared to Essie. "I just got a little bump on my noggin."

"Yes," said Opal. "Lester jumped on top of her . . ."

"What?" asked Marjorie, "You mean he attacked her sexually?"

"No, Marjorie," said Essie with disgust. "He jumped on me to protect me from an incoming firecracker. He saved my life—evidently. I don't remember a thing."

"He save your life, Essie? You mean he's a hero? I always knew it."

"What do you mean you *always* knew he was a hero, Marjorie?" sneered Opal. "You just got through saying he attacked Essie sexually."

"I like the hero story much better," said Marjorie with a smile.

"So do I." Opal chuckled through her tears. "It's much more in keeping with his character. I've known that man for many years and he would never do anything to hurt anyone. It doesn't surprise me that in the face of danger, he risked his own life to protect that of another."

"Sounds like Opal is smitten," said Essie, looking up at her two friends from her position on the grass. "Now, Opal, tell me again just what happened."

"I told you, Essie, this firecracker was headed directly towards you. Lester saw it coming and he leaped on top of you to protect you. That knocked over your chair and the both of you tipped over backwards, so Lester got the full effect of the firecracker on his . . . buttocks . . . and you got a bump when your head hit the ground. Essie, please don't make me say 'buttocks' again."

At that point, the two EMTs returned, along with Felix Federico.

"Miss Essie," said Felix, "we're so sorry about what happened to you here. The EMTs tell me that they want to take you to the hospital for the night, just to run some tests to be sure you're okay."

"Oh, fish tish," said Essie. "I don't need to go to the hospital. I'm fine. I told you. I just have a little bump. If someone will just help me up off this damp grass, I'll just go back to my room." She pushed down on the ground in an attempt to lift herself up with little success.

"Sorry, Miss Essie," repeated Felix, "I agree with the EMTs. And Happy Haven, we would be derelict in our duties if we did not follow their suggestion. It's just for the overnight. You will be back home first thing tomorrow."

Opal and Marjorie, glancing at Felix, and seeing his normally happy face so stern, nodded their agreement too.

"We'll save you a cinnamon bun from tomorrow's breakfast, Essie," promised Marjorie.

"Please, Essie, just to be safe," pleaded Opal.

"Oh, all right," Essie agreed. "Take me away!" She held out her arms. The EMTs said they'd be back in a minute with a gurney to get Essie. While they were waiting, Essie asked, "Do they have any news on Lester? I'd like to thank him for saving my life."

"All we know is that he's at the hospital," said Opal.

"Maybe you'll be in the same room," offered Marjorie, with a twinkle in her eye. "Sorry, Opal. I know he's yours."

"He is not *mine*," replied Opal. "But, Essie, if you *are* at the hospital, maybe you'll be able to find out something about his condition . . ."

"I'll do my best, Opal," replied Essie, placing her hand on Opal's arm. It was quite obvious that Opal was more than worried about her new/old friend.

"Felix, have they said anything to you about Lester's—I mean, Mr. Mills' condition?"

"No, they haven't, Opal," replied Felix, placing an arm around Opal's shoulders. "We probably won't hear anything until tomorrow, but I promise you that when I do, I will let you know first thing."

"Thank you, sir," said Opal, her shoulders shaking.

"No *sir*, please, Opal," said the manager. "Just Felix. You ladies should probably get inside soon. Oh, and where is Fay?" The women pointed to where Fay was sitting in her wheelchair. Felix wandered over and knelt down beside their companion. He talked softly to Fay as Opal and Marjorie continued to encourage Essie.

"Don't worry, Essie," said Marjorie, "Reardon Hospital has really good breakfasts."

"Oh, Marjorie," replied Essie. "I don't care about that."

"You'll be back before you know it, Essie," added Opal, "and you don't want to play around with concussion. You were unconscious, you know. You could have a concussion. They're just being extra careful. You need someone monitoring you overnight."

"Yes, yes. I get it," said Essie. The EMTs had just returned with the folding gurney.

"All right, now, Miss Essie," said the man, "let's get you on here." They lowered the gurney to the ground and both EMTs working together helped Essie to slide onto the smooth plastic surface. Essie breathed a sigh of relief to be off the damp grass and onto something dry at least. Opal and Marjorie surrounded her, and Felix rolled Fay over as the EMTs pushed Essie towards the ambulance which was waiting with an open back door in the street. The group followed Essie on her short trip to the ambulance, waving supportively as they went.

"Take care, Essie!" they all yelled. "You'll be fine!"

Essie waved back weakly with a little hand gesture. As soon as she was securely tucked into the ambulance, and they had started to drive off, she looked up at the female EMT who was sitting with her and said, "Okay, now, I want the real story of what happened. I have a head wound and the man who saved me was hit in the rear by a firecracker. Just how in blue blazes did that happen?"

Chapter 8

Almost as fast as that firecracker had knocked her off her chair, Essie now found herself all ensconced in a hospital bed at Reardon General, wearing a flimsy, revealing short gown, with nurses and orderlies fussing over her. There was really not much she hated more than people prodding and poking her with needles and other devices. They patched up her scraped head and no sooner had they shoved her into a nice cold hospital bed with a nice uncomfortable mattress, than some young aide arrived to drag her down to X-ray to have her head photographed for a concussion. *Oh, criminy!* she thought, *at least I'm off that horrible wet grass!* She watched the walls of the hospital zoom by as she was pushed rapidly to the X-Ray department for either an x-ray or a cat scan or both—she couldn't remember. The whole procedure of photographing her head only took a few minutes and then the young aide helped her back on the rolling gurney and they were off again to her awaiting hospital room.

"What time is it?" Essie asked the young man.

"Ma'am, it's 11:47 p.m.," replied the aide as he neatly rolled her around a corner without so much as slowing down. Essie wondered how he managed to look at his wristwatch. He surely hadn't removed a hand from the gurney and still exacted that turn with such finesse. She contemplated a race against him with her walker. "Don't worry," he continued. "We'll get you back to your room soon and you can get some sleep."

"Sleep," said Essie. "How does anyone expect me to sleep with everyone always poking me with needles and driving me all over this place?"

The young man chuckled. Obviously, this was a common complaint. They entered a large elevator and soon came out on a patient floor with a nurses' station. *The place is humming for 11:47 p.m.* thought Essie, but then, it *was* a hospital and it *was* the Fourth of July. She was probably not the only person who'd been involved in a fireworks accident.

Her aide rolled her into her room and over to her bed. He helped her crawl onto the crunchy plastic surface. Essie tried unsuccessfully to cover her rear end as she got into bed, but the gown barely connected in the back. The aide didn't seem to notice or care. Finally, she was situated in her bed and the aide pulled the covers up and around her gently and then he was on his way.

As Essie glanced up, she realized that she wasn't alone. A man and a woman, both dressed in street clothes were seated in chairs by the window. They rose at the same time. The woman went over and shut the door to the room and returned. They stood together formally by the side of Essie's bed.

"Mrs. Cobb?" asked the man. He was a muscular African-American with a bald head and a thick mustache. "We're from the Reardon Police Department. I'm Detective Blake and this is my partner, Detective Farley." He gestured to the slight, bespectacled woman beside him with blond hair that was only partially tied back in a knot, who glanced up from her notebook just briefly enough to give Essie a warm smile. "We'd like to ask you some questions about the *accident* that occurred tonight at the Happy Haven Retirement Center."

Essie was suddenly concerned with the addition of the police to the situation. Her thoughts went haywire. *What did this mean? Had Lester Mills died?*

"Is this about Mr. Mills?" she asked the detectives. "Is he okay? I heard they took him here after the accident. How is he?"

"We can't answer that, Ms. Cobb," said the woman. "Mr. Mills is still unconscious so we're unable to question him . . ."

"But we'd like to ask you a few questions, if you feel up to talking to us. . ." added the man, in a deep, growly voice. He sniffed noisily and rubbed his mustache.

"Of course," said Essie, mystified, "but I don't see why the police are involved in this. I mean, I assume one of the firecrackers from the city display went off-target and hit Lester, I mean, Mr. Mills . . ."

"We don't know that," explained Detective Blake. "We're just getting started on this investigation, but our preliminary information seems to indicate that Mr. Mills was struck with a firework of some sort that *didn't* come from the city display."

"What do you mean?" asked Essie. "Where else would it have come from?"

"That's a good question," said the female detective––Farley. Her voice was the extreme opposite of her partner's—soft, gentle. "And that's what we want to ask you. What did you see? Ms. Cobb, can you just tell us what you remember? Anything you remember, please."

"About the firecracker—nothing," replied Essie. "I had just come out of the building. It was dark and there were a lot of residents on the lawn. Some were milling about and some were seated in lawn chairs waiting for the fireworks display to begin. I was looking for my friends, Opal and Marjorie and Fay. We're tablemates, you see. That means, we always eat our meals together . . ."

"Yes, ma'am," said Blake, roughly, "now about the firecracker . . ."

"As I said," continued Essie, "I was looking for my friends. I had wandered far away from the building and there wasn't much light, so I couldn't see anyone very well. Then I heard my friend Opal call out to me. I moved closer to the sound of her voice and saw her sitting in a lawn chair next to Lester, I mean, Mr. Mills. You see, Opal knows Mr. Mills from years ago. He used to be a client at the tax firm where she used to work. He just came to live at Happy Haven recently and she was so surprised to see him here."

"Yes, ma'am," said Farley. Her gentleness was soothing to Essie.

"The firecracker, ma'am?" interrupted Blake.

"I'm getting there!" cried Essie. If she was going to tell a story, she was going tell it in her own way. "Anyway, I heard Opal call me, and I saw her and Lester sitting next to each other. Fay was there too, on the other side of Opal but not so close. I walked over to them. That was when Mr. Mills stood up and offered me his seat so that I could sit next to Opal. Oh, you see, I use a walker, so I had to push it over. Then Mr. Mills stood and helped me into his chair. He placed my walker close to the chair. He was just starting to stand up, and I noticed he looked up, sort of over my head and his face changed all of a sudden. Then, before I knew what was happening, he leaped on top of me and knocked me and the chair over backwards. That was the last thing I remember before I woke up and those two EMTs were poking around on me." She grimaced as she remembered the thorough prodding she'd received at their hands.

"Do you have any idea what he saw or if he saw anything?" asked Blake, staring intently into her eyes. Essie realized that whatever had happened and whatever Lester Mills had seen that had caused him to leap on her had now become a matter for the police. She needed to give careful answers. "No," she said sincerely, trying to remember. "I have no idea. I was looking at his face, but he was definitely looking above my head and whatever he saw—obviously, the firecracker—caused him to act immediately and jump on top of me. He saved my life. Or at least that's what everyone kept telling me."

"Oh, Ms. Cobb, there's no doubt Mr. Mills saved your life," said Detective Farley softly. "He's a hero."

"I'm sure when you ask *him*, he'll tell you all of this," said Essie, smiling.

"Yes," agreed Blake, glancing at his partner. "However, that's the problem. Mr. Mills is unconscious and the doctors here aren't certain when or *if* he'll be awake."

"What?" cried Essie. "He's still unconscious?"

"Yes, ma'am," replied Farley.

"I thought he was struck in the . . . uh, rear end."

"Yes, ma'am, he was. But his wounds are quite severe. He was burned quite badly. They have him in an induced coma, so there's no way, at least at the moment, for us to interrogate him."

"I see," said Essie. She felt her heart pounding. A man she barely knew had risked his life to save hers and now he was somewhere here in this very hospital clinging to life. All of a sudden, she felt very petty for worrying about her own comfort and discomfort.

"And, detectives, may I ask, why are the police involved in all of this?" asked Essie. "Isn't it just a horrible accident?"

"It might be. *If* it turns out that one of the city firecrackers went astray, it would be accidental. In that case, it's possible that Mr. Mills or his family might file a negligence lawsuit against the city. In either case, it falls to us to determine exactly what happened."

"What do you mean *if* a firecracker went astray?" asked Essie. "What else could have happened?"

"It's probably quite unlikely," suggested Farley, "but even though Reardon has a strict no-fireworks policy except for the city-approved one, sometimes, teenagers and young kids do set off illegal firecrackers in deserted locations in the community."

"Oh," replied Essie, her entire demeanor changed. "Do you think that's what happened to Mr. Mills?"

"Possibly," replied Blake. "We have a lot more investigating to do before we can make a definitive determination. And to that end, Ms. Cobb, as you don't remember what happened after Mr. Mills toppled you over, and obviously, we cannot interview him as he is in a coma, could you possibly give us the names of those other individuals who you say were seated with Mr. Mills when you joined them last night?"

"Oh, of course," said Essie. "Opal was seated with Mr. Mills. And Fay was there too. They both would have seen the accident. They would be the ones to talk to. Although, you won't get much information from Fay; she doesn't speak."

"She doesn't speak?" asked Farley, brushing her blond hair from her face. "Is she mute?"

"We don't really know," answered Essie. "I'm pretty sure she understands, though. You might find some way to question her as I'm sure she saw what happened."

Essie gave the detectives Opal's and Fay's last names and their apartment numbers at Happy Haven and the two detectives said their farewells and left.

It was now after midnight. Essie could see this clearly by the hands of the large clock on the wall directly across from her bed. She contemplated sleeping but the lights from the machines in the hospital room and the noises from people in the hallway were not conducive to rest. But most of all, Essie couldn't think of sleep because she was now extremely concerned about poor Lester Mills, lying somewhere in this very hospital, unconscious. She suddenly felt the need to go to him and express her gratitude, even though she knew that he couldn't hear her as he was in an "induced coma."

"No time like the present," Essie said out loud to no one. She grabbed the nurse call buzzer on the cord by her bed and gave it a push. All of a sudden, a voice came to her through the intercom.

"May I help you?" asked a bodiless voice.

"Where is Mr. Mills' room?" asked Essie.

"Ma'am, I'm sorry but I wouldn't know that. I'm a floor nurse. Is there anything I can do for you?"

"Well, if someone wanted to visit a patient here, how would they find out what room that patient was in?" asked Essie. Maybe a more general question would elicit a usable answer.

"Oh, they simply call the main switchboard," said the nurse.

Essie thanked the nurse and reached over to the landline phone on her nightstand. She stretched her hand out as far as she could but she couldn't reach the telephone. Maybe her grandson Ned was right. A smart phone in her pocket would come in very handy right now. She scooted her bottom closer to the nightstand and was eventually able to reach the receiver on the phone.

"She lifted the receiver and hit zero. An operator answered, "Reardon General Hospital. May I help you?"

"What room is Lester Mills in?" she asked again.

"Visiting hours are over for the day," replied the friendly voice.

"Oh, I wouldn't visit him until tomorrow," lied Essie.

"Very well," said the operator, "Lester Mills is in Room 437."

"Thank you," said Essie, hanging up. She glanced up at the door of her room; it was 233. Lester was probably two floors above her down the hall from where her room would be. She looked around. At the moment, no nurse was in her room. She scooted over to the side of the bed. Luckily, the ambulance EMTs had brought her walker with them and had deposited it in her room. She slid out of bed and scooted over to grab her trusty steed. Inside her basket, some nurse had left her sweater and her clothes. Quickly as she could, Essie slipped on her slacks and top and shoved her feet into her sneakers without her socks. She knew she was only half-dressed, but she only needed enough clothing on to not cause anyone to stare at her. Sliding quickly to the door, she peeked out. The floor was basically deserted. There was one nurse at the station but her back was turned away because she was working on a computer. Essie quickly exited her room and headed towards the elevator. As she pushed the elevator button, the machine jerked into life and quickly arrived and opened its door. Essie slid noiselessly into the elevator and pressed the button for the fourth floor. The door shut.

Chapter 9

Essie had had years of experience scooting silently around Happy Haven with her walker. She could go slowly like an octopus just rolling gently along on the ocean bottom. Or she could zip around like a squirrel, running from one maple tree to the other, so fast you could barely see it whip by you, until there he was just sitting there, nibbling on his big acorn. Now, she was that bottom-dweller, sliding and oozing along the silent hospital floor, holding tight to the walls so that no one might see her as she passed through the late-night corridors.

She'd exited the elevator on the fourth floor and had luckily found that unit's nurse's station also quiet as the lone nurse, faced away from the elevator, was focused totally on her computer too. Essie rolled her walker softly along the floor and around the corridor. Once she'd turned the corner and was out of view of the main station nurse, she cautiously peeked down the hallway, only to find it empty. She quickly picked up her speed and rushed on past the doors numbered 430, 431, 432, and so on until she reached 437, which she'd been informed was the room where Lester Mills was.

When she got there, the door was closed, but not entirely shut. Essie pushed it open a bit, listening to see if there were any nurses inside. There were none. She rolled into the room and quickly turned and shut the door behind her. Inside the room, she could see a hospital bed and a man lying in it. Although no overhead fixture was on, glow from the machines attached to the man provided enough light to see. Essie rolled over to the bed. A chart attached to the foot of the bed read "Mills, Lester." The man's lower half was covered in bandages and his upper half was attached to various cords and tubes. An oxygen mask was wrapped around his head with tubing shoved into his nostrils. The man's eyes were closed, but he appeared to be breathing deeply and on his own.

Essie rolled over. She stood there for a while just looking down at the man who had saved her life.

"I don't know you, Mr. Mills," she whispered, "but I just wanted to say thanks for saving me." Now she felt totally stupid for even being here, talking to a man who was unconscious. The nurses on her floor were now probably worried about where she was, she realized, but she found she just couldn't turn around and leave. She felt she needed to do something else. She didn't know what, so she rolled around to the far side of the bed and plopped down in a chair that had been placed close to the head of the bed. The sound of the unconscious man's gentle breathing was actually very relaxing and within minutes, Essie found herself drifting off.

"Keep quiet!" she thought she heard a voice say.

"There's no one around. Just one nurse at the station," replied another.

Where were those voices coming from?

"Get in here," said the first voice, "before someone sees you!"

Essie heard a door squeak open and then close. No, she wasn't dreaming this. It sounded like two people were moving closer to her.

"Oh, sorry," said the woman. "We didn't know anyone was . . ." Sounds of the woman and her partner scurrying away followed.

Essie's eyes suddenly popped open. *Had that really happened or did she just dream those two people coming in and out of Lester's room?*

She was puzzling over this conundrum when a nurse entered, blocking the door open with a stop. The nurse was carrying blood pressure monitoring equipment. Her short platinum hair was tipped with purple and Essie couldn't help but wonder if she'd recently bent too low over a pan of medicine and accidentally gotten it dyed. The young woman started over to the patient, obviously to take a regular reading, when she saw Essie sitting on the opposite side of the bed.

"Oh, my! Who are you?" she asked, stopping in her tracks, her big violet eyes that matched the ends of her hair, widening. Lester Mills remained sound asleep.

"Um," replied Essie, "I'm Essie. This is Lester. He saved my life tonight. I just wanted to come up and thank him." She gave the nurse her most charming smile.

"Oh," replied the nurse, setting her equipment down on the rolling nightstand, and coming around to where Essie was sitting. "I see. You're a patient." She glanced at Essie's sockless feet.

"Yes," said Essie. "On the second floor."

"Do they know you're up here?" she asked.

"No," said Essie with a shrug, "I sort of sneaked out."

"I bet you did," answered the nurse, shaking her head. "I bet they're looking for you too."

"You do a lot of betting, don't you?" asked Essie, fluttering her eyelashes sweetly.

"Well, don't you worry about that," suggested the nurse. "Why don't we just get you back to your room. I'm sure second floor will be all flustered . . ."

"You mean because they *lost* a patient?" offered Essie innocently.

"Have you been in this hospital before, Miss . . . Miss . . . "

"Cobb," she replied, "Essie Cobb."

"Essie Cobb," said the petite nurse, scrunching up her face. "You know, I think I've heard of you."

"Of me?"

"Yes, you. I believe I read about you in the newspaper once. Haven't you solved a mystery or something like that?" She pointed a sparkly purple fingernail at Essie.

"I have," said Essie, nodding. Local reporters were always pestering her about her investigations. "I've actually solved a few. And I was just thinking about solving this one."

"Which one?"

"The one involving Mr. Mills here."

"Oh, and how is it a mystery?" asked the young nurse, going back to her blood pressure cuff and quickly attaching it to her patient.

"Mr. Mills risked his life tonight to save me from an incoming firecracker," explained Essie.

"That was nice of him," replied the nurse, writing down the blood pressure results on her chart and wrapping up the cuff. "But how is that a mystery?"

"For one thing," said Essie, "we were quite a distance from the fireworks display. If anyone was going to be hit by one of those things, you wouldn't think it would come all the way out to Happy Haven."

"Happy Haven Retirement Center?" asked the nurse, returning to Essie and positioning the walker in front of her.

"Yes."

"You know, I believe I did hear someone mention that. But things just got so busy—the holidays, and everything. My grandma lives at Happy Haven. That *is* quite a distance. I mean, not to *see* the fireworks. But for a firecracker to travel all that way . . ." She placed one of her purple nails to her mouth.

"Yes—a mystery. See!"

"I do, Miss Essie, but I'm afraid you're going to have to solve it back on the second floor." She gave her a scowl and Essie rose reluctantly, leaning on her walker.

"Oh, nurse," Essie asked, "just before you came in, did you see two people coming out of this room? A young woman and someone else?"

"No, I didn't see anyone. It's much too late for visitors."

"Well, I think they were here in this room just before you came in," Essie declared with more firmness than she felt. "Then when they saw me, they turned around and left. It was strange."

"Are you sure about that? It's really late, Miss Essie, and it sounds as if you've had quite an emotional day. Maybe you're just imagining things."

"Maybe," admitted Essie, thinking she might have dozed off. She wasn't exactly certain if the two people had really been there or if it all had been part of a dream.

"But, Ms. Essie, you're diverting me from helping you get back to your room. If you're a patient here, I hardly think your doctor wants you roaming around the hospital late at night."

"Oh, all right," said Essie. "I'll go back." She gave her walker a shove and started out of the room.

"Oh, no, you don't, young lady!" said the nurse, stopping Essie by standing in front of her, her hand raised. "I'm going to *escort* you back down to the second floor myself, and report you in to the head nurse there, and make sure she knows you like to wander about. We can't have any more of this kind of escapade."

"You're no fun," scowled Essie, "I'll never solve any mysteries if everyone is a spoil sport like you. By the way, who are you?"

"I'm Francine," said the young woman. "Glad to meet you."

"Likewise," replied Essie. "I like all your purple . . . uh . . . well, I like all of your purple parts."

"Thanks!" said the nurse, glancing at her nails and breathing on her fingertips with a flourish before she patted Essie's hand.

The young nurse escorted Essie to the elevator and down to the second floor. When she walked her over to the nurses' station, the nurse on duty was flabbergasted to see her.

"Mrs. Cobb!" she cried. "Where have you been? We've been looking all over the floor for you!"

"Oh, I just took a little walk, dearie," said Essie, producing her *sweet as cotton candy* smile. "This purple nurse, I mean, Francine here helped me find my way back."

"I found her in a patient's room," reported Francine to her colleague. "I suggest you keep an eye on this one. Says she's out to solve a mystery."

"You'll just have to solve your mystery later, my dear. Right now, I'm going to get you back to your bed. Your doctor would be furious if he knew you were gallivanting around all over the place," said the head nurse.

"Take care," said Francine to her colleague as she headed back into the elevator. "Good luck, Ms. Cobb!" She waved her purple fingers as the doors closed on her. Essie waved back, but the head nurse was guiding her back to her room.

"Oh, nurse, how often do people visit patients in the middle of the night?" asked Essie as they walked back to Room 232.

"It depends," answered the older nurse. "We sometimes have relatives take up residence to be with a patient. Husbands with wives or parents with children. Depends on how sick the patient is. Other things."

"Well, this patient is in a coma and I think two people came into his room in the middle of the night, and then turned around and left when they saw me."

"You mean the man you were visiting up on the fourth floor?"

"Yes, that one."

"Maybe they thought you were a nurse and they knew they shouldn't be there so late."

"Would you mistake me for a nurse?" Essie asked her incredulously, pointing to her walker and sockless feet.

"No," said the older woman truthfully.

"Then why just come in and go right out again?"

"You scared them?"

"Me? Me? Scared them? How? I'm a helpless little old lady."

"I have no idea. But it was probably just confusing for them to see someone else—anyone else—sitting there in the room."

"I would think that if anything, they'd be curious and want to know why I was there or go get a nurse and find out what I was doing there. But they just took one look at me and left—no questions asked."

"People are strange. Are you sure you really saw these people?"

"Maybe not. I think I did doze off for a while. I may have dreamt it all."

The nurse helped Essie crawl back into her hospital bed and then pulled the covers up over her and tucked her in. "Try to get some sleep, Ms. Cobb. It will be morning before you know it."

"One can only hope," grinned Essie. The hospital bed was the hardest, lumpiest piece of furniture that she'd ever laid her head on. Morning couldn't come soon enough.

Chapter 10

Essie got absolutely no sleep that night. In addition to the lumpy hospital bed, the nurses came in to check on her probably even more frequently than they would have any other patient—no doubt because of her late night stroll. Of course, they said they just wanted to make certain she hadn't suffered a concussion, but Essie suspected that they didn't trust her. She was itching to get out of there and back to Happy Haven.

In the morning, after a totally boring and tasteless hospital breakfast, she attempted to dress herself with her clothes from yesterday that were still in the basket of her walker that had now been placed further away from her bed—obviously, another ploy of the nurses to prevent her from walking about. She had to hang onto the edge of the bed and walls to get to her walker and bring it back. Getting her clothes on without help was more than difficult. Her old body just didn't bend in the ways necessary to get legs easily into pants and arms into shirts.

Nevertheless, she was dressed and ready to go when one of the morning crew nurses popped in, cheerful as could be. Obviously, that was because the nurse had been able to sleep in her own comfortable bed.

"Well, look at you!" said the friendly woman, "Looks like you're ready to go home."

"I've been *ready* for some time," declared Essie with a huff, sitting on the edge of her bed, a firm grip on the handles of her walker, in case someone tried to separate them again. "When can I get out of here?"

"The doctor will have to sign you out, dear," replied the nurse. "He's on his rounds now. He should be here soon. Be patient." She came over to Essie in an attempt to fluff her pillow, but Essie held up her hand.

"I'm fine. I'll just sit here and wait for him." She waved the woman away. The nurse left quietly, closing the door behind her.

All of a sudden, the door to her room flung open, and her daughters Prudence and Claudia stormed in.

"Mom!" cried the younger daughter Claudia, coming over to her, "why didn't you call me or have someone call and tell me that you were in the hospital?" She hugged Essie and proceeded to look her over.

"Oh, Mom," added the older and taller Prudence on Essie's other side, "what happened to your head? They said something about you being hit by a firecracker? Oh, my Lord!" Prudence examined the gauze bandage that was wrapped around Essie's head.

"Oh, look at the size of that bandage. Why on earth didn't they call us?" snapped Claudia. The two sisters were now in full hysteria mode, fussing over Essie and bemoaning the failure of the system that hadn't notified them of their mother's accident.

"I'm fine, girls," said Essie, trying to calm her daughters as the two women prodded and examined her. "They just brought me here to make sure I didn't have a concussion . . ."

"Concussion!" cried Claudia.

"I was unconscious for just a bit . . ." admitted Essie with a little grin.

"Unconscious," said Pru, "Oh my, Mom. This is serious."

"No, dear, it's not; I'm fine. The doctor will be here shortly to release me. Neither one of you needed to come. I didn't call you because I knew you'd just hurry over here for nothing. *Actually,* thought Essie, *I didn't call my daughters as I knew they'd do just what they're doing now—make a fuss.* She spoke up clearly, "As soon as the doctor says I can go, I'm going back to Happy Haven."

"Goodness, Mom, what happened?" asked Claudia.

"Actually, it was rather amusing," said Essie, attempting to calm her daughters' building concern. "I was just watching the fireworks' display on the front lawn at Happy Haven when all of a sudden one of the residents jumped on top of me. That was all I remembered. When I regained consciousness, I found out that he'd seen a firecracker heading right at me and he jumped on top of me to protect me. Now, isn't that funny?" She giggled and gave her daughters a cheesy grin.

"Some man jumped on you?" gasped Pru.

"To protect me!" cried Essie.

"Couldn't he just have pulled you out of the way?" asked Claudia.

"Girls," stated Essie firmly, "I was seated. The firecracker was heading right towards the back of my head. Lester, I mean, Mr. Mills, was standing facing me. I don't see any other way he could have gotten me out of harm's way except for what he did. He's a hero. How can you question his motives?"

"It just seems a little inappropriate," said Pru, hinting at scandal. "Men jumping on women at a retirement center." She pulled at a tuft on her sweater and sniffed.

"You should know, that his actions resulted in him being direly injured himself. He's here now on the fourth floor—in a coma."

"Oh, my!" said Claudia. "Do they expect him to survive?"

"I don't know about that," replied Essie, "but he was evidently badly injured when the firecracker struck him in the . . . behind."

"We're sorry, Mom," said Prudence. "I guess we owe this . . . Mills fellow . . ."

"Lester," offered Essie.

"Yes, Lester," said Claudia.

"We owe this Lester Mills a debt of gratitude for protecting you," continued Prudence. "Claudia, you and I should go visit him."

"Yes!" cried Essie, "you should. And, while you're up there, would you keep a look out for his children?" She started to rise to shoo her busybody daughters out the door.

"His children?" asked Claudia.

"Yes," said Essie. "I'm . . . uh, not sure, but I believe he has two boys and a girl. I believe I've seen them with him around Happy Haven. I don't know if anyone has contacted them. They must be . . . uh, terribly upset. If you see them up there, please let them know how grateful I am to their father." Essie rose, hanging onto her walker in an attempt to get her daughters to leave.

"We will, Mom, but first we're going to deal with you. If they're going to release you, we'll just wait here until they do and then take you home," said Prudence.

"They said I have to wait for the doctor to examine me and sign my release papers," Essie said. "Maybe you two could go up to the fourth floor and check in on Mr. Mills and then come back here and let me know how he's doing . . ."

"Why?" asked Claudia. "I doubt that there's much we could find out about his condition, and if he's in a coma, we obviously can't speak to him."

"Besides," added Pru, "I think we should wait here with you so we can speak to the doctor ourselves to be certain you're okay."

"Agreed," said Claudia. "You are our main priority. Mr. Mills will just have to wait until we take care of you."

At that moment, a doctor followed by two nurses carrying charts entered Essie's room like a royal entourage. All conversation and movement stopped.

"Ms., uh, Cobb!" announced the doctor, glancing down at Essie's chart. His eyes quickly perused the medical jargon on the various sheets and then looked up at her and smiled. "So, it seems as if you want to go home."

"I do, doctor," replied Essie.

"Well, then, let's get you out of here. I don't see any indication of concussion. You did lose consciousness for some time, so we did a CT scan just to be safe. But all tests look normal and everything else checks out."

"Thank you, doctor," replied Essie, not adding anything else for fear of jeopardizing her forthcoming release.

"Are you sure, doctor?" interjected Claudia. "I mean, I understand she was tackled by a man at her retirement home last night . . ."

"And she was unconscious for some time," added Pru.

Thanks, daughters, thought Essie. *Now I'll never get out of here.*

"Let's check," replied the doctor, doing a quick glance back at the chart. "How's that head?" he asked Essie, pulling back the gauze bandage and poking at her injury.

"Just a little sore, doctor," replied Essie in her most agreeable patient voice.

"Well, it's certainly not sufficient reason to keep you here," he concluded. "Let's get her on her way," he said to the two nurses, as he quickly scrawled his signature onto the bottom of the top paper. "Good luck, Ms.

Cobb, and watch out for those firecrackers!" He turned and exited swiftly, followed by one nurse. The other nurse remained and began to give directions to Essie and her daughters. Soon, everything had been accomplished and Claudia and Prudence were escorting their mother and her walker out of the Reardon General Hospital and into Claudia's van, which was parked in the attached garage.

"You know who I'm mad at?" asked Claudia to no one in particular. "I'm mad at Happy Haven. They should have contacted us when you were taken to the hospital, Mom." She started her engine and rolled out into the winding garage.

"In all fairness, Claudia," responded the older Prudence, "if this happened as late at night as Mom says, they probably didn't have anyone there to make a call . . ."

"That's ridiculous," snapped Claudia. "There's always someone there. I'm thinking I'll lodge a complaint." She held onto the steering wheel with one hand while reaching into a side pocket of her purse with the other for her cell phone. She quickly pressed a button on the device as she swung out of the garage and into street traffic.

"Now, girls," said Essie, the whole episode starting to remind her of how the two sisters used to fight over everything when they were little. One would take a stand and the other would invariably take the other side. Since Essie had moved into Happy Haven, it had seemed as if they were always ganging up on *her* now. "Let's not jump the gun here. You know, if I get back soon enough, maybe the dining hall will still be open and I can get breakfast . . ." Essie wondered out loud.

"Didn't they feed you at the hospital, Mom?" Prudence was aghast. "You need to eat!"

"Yes!" agreed Claudia, now diverted from her original fury over not being called when Essie was admitted to the hospital and dropping her phone back into her purse. "What is wrong with that place? Pru, we can't rely on her getting anything to eat at Happy Haven."

"I know," agreed Prudence. "They've probably closed down their breakfast service by now." The older sister glanced at her wristwatch and announced, "It's almost ten."

"I know!" shouted Claudia, and with a twirl of the steering wheel, she made a left at the next corner and soon the threesome had pulled into the parking lot of a local eatery.

"How about this?" asked Claudia. She put the van in park and turned around and smiled at Essie in the back seat.

"Perfect," stated Pru, her little kerfuffle with her sister now forgotten. "Are you well enough for a really good breakfast, Mom?"

"Can I have waffles with strawberry syrup?" asked Essie eagerly.

"You can have whatever you want!" both sisters exclaimed, at the same time slapping their palms together. This was the sibling behavior that Essie enjoyed seeing the most.

"I took off work to pick you up from the hospital, but the office doesn't need to know how long it took me," Claudia added with a giggle.

"And, of course, I don't need to report my activities to Marvin," added Pru who was retired, "as he doesn't care what I do."

The sisters got out, Prudence removing and unfolding Essie's walker and Claudia assisting Essie down to the ground from the van's tall back seat. The three were soon on their way inside Pancake Platter, a local eatery near Happy Haven, and a favorite of Essie's for family outings.

Essie's nose could immediately smell the delightful aroma of pancakes, bacon, and other home-baked goods that Pancake Platter was famous for. Luckily, it was mid-morning on a weekday, and the place was not terribly busy. They were seated quickly and coffee was poured all around as they waited for their orders.

"So, Mom," began Claudia, "now that you're out of the hospital and we're seated, you can tell us all about this little *accident* of yours."

"Oh, fertile feathers," said Essie, "It was nothing. Just a little knock on my noggin. Nothing to get so upset over. I'm fine."

"I may believe that you're fine physically, Mom," said Pru, "but I can certainly tell that there's more going on inside that head of yours. Now, out with it."

But, at that moment, plates piled high with pancakes and waffles were delivered to the table and all three ladies sighed and began to eat. The story of Essie's *accident* would have to wait.

Chapter 11

Essie returned to Happy Haven shortly before her assigned lunch period. Luckily, she'd spent so much time at the Pancake Platter regaling her daughters with tales of her exciting night that she hadn't eaten all of her waffle, so her stomach was already starting to rumble again. After a quick trip to the bathroom (and her shiny new toilet seat!), Essie rolled out and headed for the dining hall.

When she arrived, all three of her tablemates were already seated. When they saw her, they waved and smiled.

"Essie!" cried Marjorie, "we're so glad to see you. When they took you off to the hospital, we were so worried."

Essie plopped herself down in her chair and pulled her walker beside her.

"Essie, are you okay?" asked Opal, eyeing the bandage on Essie's head. "Did you have to have stitches?"

"No," replied Essie, touching her bandage. "It was just a scratch. I'll probably just have a bruise."

"What about a concussion?" asked Marjorie. "You *were* unconscious."

"It was all just a lot of hoopla for nothing," replied Essie, pulling herself up to the table. Fay reached across the table and grabbed Essie's hand and squeezed it. Essie looked over at her pudgy little friend and smiled. "Thank you, Fay. I'm fine. I would have been back for breakfast but it took forever to get the release forms signed, and then my daughters came and they checked me out, and then they wanted to go out for breakfast, and so we went to Pancake Platter . . ."

"Ooo!" declared Marjorie, "I like that place."

"So, what's been happening here?" asked Essie, looking around the table. Santos arrived and poured Essie some coffee. She looked quickly at the menu and pointed to an entree. "I'll have the pork chop," she said. He gave her a little nod and headed off. The other women were already eating their meals.

"Nothing much," replied Opal, "although people are talking about the accident. Not every day does a resident get hit by a firecracker . . ."

"I know," said Essie. "Believe me, it's not something I want to relive. They even sent the police to talk to me in the hospital. But I really didn't see much. I did direct them to you, Opal, because I assume that you saw what happened and, of course, they can't talk to Mr. Mills as he's still unconscious."

"Yes," said Opal, "that's fine. I'll be glad to talk to them. Poor Lester."

"So, Opal," asked Marjorie, "what *did* you see?"

"Not much," replied the tall woman, taking a deep breath. "I guess I was so shocked and it all happened so fast that I'm not really sure what I saw . . ."

"Which was what?" prodded Essie.

"I remember Lester offering you his seat," said Opal, smiling. "That was so gallant of him . . ."

"Yes, we know, Opal, he's Prince Charming," said Essie, rolling her hand in the air in an attempt to speed up Opal's tale. "Then what?"

"I walked over to Fay to check on her, I remember. Lester helped you sit down, Essie, and placed your walker nearby. Then I remember he looked up over your head and his face changed. I glanced up to where he was looking and I saw this firecracker thingy heading directly towards him—or rather towards you, Essie—and then I saw him jump on top of you, knocking you backwards in the chair just at the exact moment that the thing struck. The police said they weren't sure what it was, but it certainly looked like a firecracker to me. And it struck Lester. Oh, it was horrible! The explosion was so loud and I could feel the heat from where I was standing. I was only a few feet away. I guess I just automatically bent over Fay to protect her from getting burned."

"Did you get checked out, Opal? And Fay?" asked Marjorie. "I never thought about the two of you being so close to the explosion."

"Yes," said Opal. "We were fine. We were shaken up but neither of us was injured and neither of us passed out like Essie did. It was poor Lester who suffered the major blow." She removed her hanky from the sleeve of her sweater and dabbed at her eyes. "I can't believe this happened to him. Here he is a brand new resident at Happy Haven, and now he's in the hospital, fighting for his life. I wish I knew how he's doing."

"Well, Opal," began Essie, "I may be able to reassure you of that. I actually saw your Mr. Mills, or Lester, in the hospital." She put her finger to her lips to prevent Opal from an outburst.

"You saw him!" Opal whispered with awe.

"Yes," replied Essie. "I was so bored with just lying there last night and it was impossible to sleep, what with the lumpy bed and all the noise, so I decided to take a little walk. I sneaked out of my room and wandered up to Mr. Mills' room and sort of peeked in on him. He was unconscious, but he was breathing on his own and he looked peaceful. I sat at his bedside for a bit and thanked him for saving my life."

"Oh, Essie," declared Opal. "How did you ever manage that?"

"Truthfully," she answered, "they don't pay much attention to the patients, except when they're admitting them, releasing them, or taking their vitals. Otherwise, no one cares. I had a nice little visit with your new beau, Opal."

"He's not my beau," began Opal, then with a shrug, she began sobbing softly.

"It's okay, Opal," said Marjorie. Fay reached over and patted Opal on the shoulder.

"You know, Opal," said Essie, changing the subject, "I was thinking about Lester's children. . ."

"What about Lester's children, Essie?"

"Oh, I don't know," said Essie, "but I believe I saw them with him getting into the elevator the other day. There were two young men and a young woman."

"Yes," said Opal. "I believe he has three children. I don't remember their names, but he did speak of them from time to time when he came into the office. What did they look like?"

"I don't remember," said Essie.

"You don't remember? I thought you were this great sleuth, Essie. How can you see Lester's children and not remember what they look like?"

"I wasn't trying to remember anyone at the time. I'd say they were all in their thirties or forties, but I'm not very good with ages. All brunettes. The men were taller than the woman. . ."

"Wow, Essie," cried Marjorie, "that's not much to go on."

"Your powers of observation are really not great, Essie," said Opal, dismissively. "I expected more from Reardon's most famous amateur sleuth."

"So, Opal," inquired Essie, "if you think *my* powers of observation are so poor, what about yours? Why can't you describe what the firecracker looked like?"

"But that happened so fast," declared Opal.

"As did the entrance and exit of Lester's children into the elevator. You see, it's not so easy to recall something when you're not prepared to remember it, is it?" Essie neglected to mention that she'd also seen Lester's children close up when she'd ridden the elevator down with them later that day. "Opal, do you remember what direction the firecracker came from?"

"I'm not really sure," replied Opal. "I think the west; I guess more the northwest. I'm thinking probably from where that field is down the street, you know?" The women nodded. "Maybe it was set off by some teenage hoodlums."

"That's what the detectives suggested when they interviewed me in my hospital room. If it was set off by some young hooligans," argued Essie, "it'll be really hard to track them down now."

"That's for certain," added Marjorie. Santos arrived with Essie's pork chop and she dug in, her appetite definitely not damaged by her recent hospitalization or her recent breakfast of waffles.

"I was talking to Clarisse Delacroix at the beauty parlor this morning," said Opal, "and *she* recalled that on one of her neighborhood walks, she'd seen teenage boys playing in that open field down the block. She also said she'd heard other residents mention that they'd heard that people sometimes did use that field to shoot off illegal fireworks."

"That's horrible!" cried Marjorie. The fury in her voice and the determination on her face must have motivated Fay, who squeezed her hands together in fists and pounded on the table several times.

"My goodness, Fay," said Opal, "I've never seen you so worked up over something."

"She doesn't like injustice," said Essie, "and neither do I. I don't like to see that poor man lying unconscious in a hospital bed merely because he was being gallant and trying to protect me at the Fourth of July fireworks display."

"Well, I don't see what we can do about it," said Marjorie, calming. "Sorry, Fay. I didn't mean to upset you. But this is a problem for the police, not us."

"Oh, I don't know about that, Marjorie," said Essie. "We've been able to assist the police with some cases in the past."

"And how do you propose *we* find out who shot off these illegal fireworks, Essie, if that's what you're proposing?" demanded Opal, her brow knitting, as she rolled her necklace between her fingertips.

"By doing a little snooping," whispered Essie softly, looking around surreptitiously.

"And where would we be snooping?" asked Marjorie.

"The field, of course," replied Essie.

"Essie, I'm sure the police have checked there already. They have forensics teams for that. What could we—four old ladies—find that the police haven't located already?" demanded Opal.

"*We* have more time," said Essie. "*We* have all day, if necessary, and, besides, that field isn't that far away. Many Happy Haven residents walk down there on their daily strolls, so I'm told."

"Yes," agreed Marjorie, "but they don't go searching about in all that high grass. We'd get lost. And, Essie, how can you roll your walker around on that uneven ground with all those weeds everywhere?"

"Marjorie, I am very nimble with my walker. You'd be surprised at what I can do."

"Not avoid an incoming firecracker," suggested Opal.

"That's below the belt, Opal," said Essie, "You know that firecracker came from behind me. If I'd been facing it and if I'd been standing up and if I'd had my walker, I could have probably outrun it."

"If, if if, Essie!" cried Marjorie. Fay was starting to get excited again and shaking her fists as the women got more heated in their discussion.

"Calm down, Essie," said Opal, placing her hand gently on Essie's arm. "Let's not get poor Fay upset."

"Oh, Fay's not upset," said Essie, "She's excited. She just wants to be involved in the action. And she *will* be. There's no reason all four of us can't go search that field—unless, of course, some of you are too *chicken*!" Essie made a face at them all.

That threat stopped all further conversation because, evidently, even elderly ladies did not relish being called *chicken*.

Chapter 12

After lunch, the four pals immediately headed out to the field. (Well, not exactly *immediately*. They first all went to their rooms for potty breaks, but then they all met back in the lobby and were ready to go.)

"Should we sign out?" asked Opal as they headed towards the main entrance.

"To where? What should we list as our *destination*? To *search nearby field for signs of illegal fireworks*? No," whispered Essie. "As far as anyone here is concerned, we're just taking a nice morning stroll around the neighborhood." She gave Phyllis at the front desk a big cheesy smile as she led her investigative team outside. Opal was pushing Fay, the two of them following behind Essie and Marjorie. The ladies walked at Essie's pace, which was actually rather quick.

"Essie!" shouted Marjorie to Essie, who was rolling her walker down the sidewalk that circled around the entrance to Happy Haven and connected to the street, "Slow down! Opal and Fay can't go that fast!" Essie glanced back at her more sedate companions—one in a wheelchair—and, with a shake of her head, reduced her pace.

"We don't have all day!" she yelled back at them. She turned west, continuing onto the sidewalk.

At the end of the block, the women crossed the street with the light. Opal insisted. "I feel safer if I stay in the crosswalk with Fay," she declared. Safely on the opposite side of the street, the foursome followed the sidewalk further west, past residential houses and a few small office buildings. Finally, after crossing another side street, they arrived at a large open field that spanned a good city block. The entire area was covered in tall grass and weeds.

"I can't believe the city allows this eyesore to remain here," said Marjorie. "It's obvious they don't take care of it."

"Agreed, Marjorie," said Essie, "This field is just an invitation for hoodlums and riffraff to congregate and cause trouble."

"Come on, Essie," said Opal, pulling up the rear with Fay. She was huffing a bit, as she was pushing Fay up a slight incline. "Can we just get on with whatever it is you're going to do?" Fay looked around at the field and her three friends and clapped.

"No need to clap, Fay," said Essie, "at least, not yet. We haven't done anything so far."

"So, what's your plan?" asked Marjorie.

"I'm going to investigate," replied Essie. "Marjorie, why don't you come with me? I think it's best, Opal, if you and Fay remain here on the edge of the field. . . um, in case we have any trouble, which I'm sure we won't, but if we don't come out for a long time, then maybe you can go back to Happy Haven and get help . . ."

"What kind of trouble, Essie?" asked Opal, suddenly fearful. "And how long should we wait here? And if we go back to Happy Haven, who should we bring back?"

"Oh, skittle brittle!" cried Essie, "don't ask so many questions. I don't know. Fifteen minutes maybe. But don't worry. Nothing is going to happen. Marjorie and I are just going to search around for a while and see if we can find anything that those hoodlums who shot Lester might have dropped . . ."

"But, Essie," declared Marjorie, "surely the police have already searched . . ."

"Look at this place, Marjorie," said Essie, gesturing over the expansive field with her hand. "It's huge. Those rascals could have shot off that rocket from anywhere in there. Do you really believe the police searched everywhere—if at all?"

"I don't know, Essie, it does seem a rather daunting task," said Marjorie, shirking. "I'm not sure I'm dressed right for hacking around in and amongst those tall weeds."

"She's worried about her pretty manicure," sneered Opal.

"I am not," snorted Marjorie. "Come on, Essie. Let's go."

"More like it," replied Essie, rolling her walker along the edge of the field, looking for an opening in the weeds. "Here, Marjorie. Here's a way in." She turned her walker abruptly and disappeared into the high grass and weeds. Marjorie followed, delicately, attempting not to touch or be touched by any of the dry, pokey plants.

Leaving Opal and Fay standing guard on the sidewalk, Essie zoomed as quickly as possible towards the interior of the weeded field, Marjorie following behind her.

"Essie, these weeds are sharp," cried the red-head. "Ouch!"

"Toughen up, Marjorie," replied Essie without looking back, her eyes ahead and on the ground. She followed what appeared to be a worn-down pathway. Scooting her walker around, she forged ahead. "Look around, Marjorie. If you see anything, let me know."

"There's nothing to see, Essie, except sharp old weeds and dried grass. This is a waste of time. Let's go back."

"No way," said Essie, speeding up as she became accustomed to following the slightly worn path through the field. "Ooops. Here's a break in the path. It seems to go two different directions. I don't think we should separate, but I'd like to follow both trails. Okay. Let's try this one to the left first and then we'll come back and do the right one later." Essie veered her walker to the left and headed deeper into the tall grass. Little pieces of straw and weeds were attached to her hair now but she was oblivious to it.

Soon, the two women came out into a small clearing. There was quite a bit of human trash lying about, including used condom packets, empty beer cans, and burned-out remains of firecrackers.

"This must be where the culprits set off that rocket!" cried Marjorie. "We've found it!"

"Maybe," said Essie, looking around. "There were certainly people here—and recently. Look around, Marjorie, and see if you spy anything that might be a clue." The two women scouted the ground and surrounding brush.

Marjorie did as told and they searched the little clearing.

"There's nothing here," Essie declared. "Let's go back and try the other path."

Essie rolled her walker around and headed out the way she came in. When she reached the fork where they'd been earlier, Essie turned right and the two women headed in that direction. This path was definitely smaller and rougher.

"Are you sure this is even a path, Essie?" asked Marjorie, nettles and sticks attaching to her shirt and her hair.

"Just stay with me," ordered Essie, slowing noticeably as the weeds and grass became thicker, not thinner. Essie continued to push forward, all the while Marjorie continued to complain and demand that they return.

"We've been here long enough, Essie!" cried Marjorie. "Let's go back."

"No," said Essie. "You go back if you want, but I'm not done." Marjorie took a deep breath and stomped her feet in frustration. Just then, the weeds cleared again, and the twosome found themselves in another clearing, this one much smaller and obviously less used than the one they'd found earlier.

"No one's been here, Essie," said Marjorie, looking around. There were no trash remains strewn around as there had been in the first clearing.

"Yes, they have," said Essie, bending over and looking intently at a spot on the ground as she hung onto her walker. "Look here. The ground has been stomped on. People have been here."

"So? I'm sure lots of teenagers come out here when they want privacy. You know, young love, and all that." Marjorie waved her hands about indicating that Essie must know what she meant.

"Yes, Marjorie, I know what you mean, but I don't think young lovers would enjoy romance on the hard ground in a weed field. Kids who come out here are up to some other prank."

"Essie, you saw the used condoms back there," said Marjorie, as a reminder.

"Those could be years old. Besides, there aren't any condoms here," she noted, as she glanced around and gestured.

"What's that?" said Marjorie, all of a sudden, glancing down at the edge of the weeds. "Look, Essie!" she said, as she pulled a small piece of white paper from between some tall weeds. She unfolded the paper and read it. "It looks like somebody's homework. There's lots of notations about geometry or something."

"Let me see," said Essie, sticking her face over the paper. "It might be something. It doesn't have a name on it, unfortunately." Essie folded the paper back up and stuck it in her pocket.

"Oh, Essie," cried Marjorie again, bending down at the edge of the clearing. "Look at this!"

"What?" asked Essie. Marjorie picked up a small object and returned to Essie to show her.

"It's a woman's earring," said Marjorie, "and by the look of it, it's an expensive one, at that. I'm sure this is a real ruby in the center and it's surrounded by real diamonds."

Essie took the long, gold dangly earring in her hand. "Are you sure?"

"Essie, if there's one thing I *know*, it's jewelry," replied Marjorie. "This isn't something some teenage girl would wear."

"Hmm," said Essie. "We don't know that."

"No, it's an assumption, but a fairly safe one," replied Marjorie. "Most young girls wear *Hello, Kitty* earrings and such."

"I guess we could get it appraised."

"Or give it to the police," replied Marjorie, "They're the ones searching for clues."

"And they didn't do a very good job of it, did they?" asked Essie. "I mean, we found it."

"You mean, I found it."

"Yes, yes, you found it," answered Essie. "And it's a very good clue, Marjorie."

"Essie, it may have nothing whatsoever to do with that rocket that struck Lester Mills."

"Yes, but, then again, it may. I'm taking it. It's a clue."

"Yes, ma'am, Detective Essie," replied Marjorie, as Essie pocketed the earring.

"Don't be sassy, Marjorie," said Essie. "This is serious. Now keep looking." Marjorie sighed and continued to search the edge of the clearing, looking for any other items that might provide a clue to the identity of the person who'd shot the firecracker that had struck Lester Mills the night of the Fourth.

After a while, the two women decided that they'd located all the possible clues that existed. Essie motioned for Marjorie to follow her, and she headed off down the original path that had led them into the field. After a while, they emerged suddenly onto the sidewalk next to the street. Glancing down the block, they saw Opal and Fay coming their way.

"Essie!" cried Opal. "Thank God you two are okay! We were just about ready to go back. A police cruiser has been by at least twice now. Each time, the officer has stared at us."

"He just probably wondered what two old ladies were doing standing on the street by the edge of an old field," said Essie calmly.

"You think?" asked Opal, hands waving frantically. "I was afraid he'd stop and demand that we tell him what we were doing here."

"Just say you were taking a walk."

"But Essie, we weren't walking. We were just standing there in front of this old overgrown field. We couldn't look any more suspicious if we were holding firecrackers in our hands."

"Moonies petunies!" shouted Essie. "Instead of standing here screaming about it, let's just turn around and head back to Happy Haven before he drives by again." She turned on her heels and headed the other direction towards Happy Haven. Opal pushed Fay, following Essie, and Marjorie brought up the rear.

When the women finally returned back to Happy Haven, and were safely inside the lobby, Essie said, "Now there, Opal, see. No police cruiser followed us."

"What a complete waste of time," declared Opal. "My nerves have been shot for nothing."

"Not nothing," said Essie. "Let's sit down. Marjorie and I want to show you something." The four women quickly found comfy seats in the lobby.

Essie reached into her pocket and pulled out the piece of homework paper and the gold earring.

"Clues," whispered Essie as she held out the items for the other two women to see.

"What's that?" asked Opal, looking at the paper. She took it from Essie and examined it. "It's just some teenager's geometry assignment." She picked up the earring from Essie's other hand. "And some woman dropped an earring. So what? How do these two things help us figure out who shot that rocket at Lester?"

"Opal," said Essie, holding up her hand to calm her friend. "Any good detective knows that you don't always know how a clue fits a puzzle. We don't know how this paper and this earring fit now, but we do know that they are items that you wouldn't expect to find out in a weed field where probably a firecracker was launched that almost killed someone. We just have to keep investigating until we figure it out. And that's what we're going to do. But look at the bright side. At least, now we have some clues to work with."

Chapter 13

At that moment, a man and a woman walked into the main entrance. The man walked up to the front desk and gestured to Phyllis.

"Oh, shifty fifty!" whispered Essie to her friends, gesturing subtly to the two people over at the desk.

"What?" asked Marjorie, adopting Essie's surreptitious tone.

"Don't look at those two," ordered Essie, and Opal and Marjorie immediately glanced at the couple.

"Nice going, Opal," replied Essie. "That's those two detectives who interviewed me at the hospital."

"Oh no!" cried Opal. "Do you think they found out about us searching the field?"

"How could they?" Marjorie asked, also whispering. "We just got back from there." The three pals were now sitting close together with their heads almost touching. Fay, obviously anxious to join the excitement, bent over in her wheelchair too.

Essie glanced over at the black man who was now talking in an animated fashion to Phyllis. Phyllis just then looked over at Essie and her friends sitting in the lobby and pointed the women out to the detective.

"Oh no!" cried Opal again. "Phyllis has ratted us out."

"I doubt that, Opal," replied Marjorie. "Phyllis has no idea what we've been doing."

The two detectives headed straight over to the group of women.

"Miss Cobb," said the man. "I'm happy to see you've been released from the hospital."

"Yes, um, Mr. . . um?"

"Blake, Detective Blake, and this is my partner, Detective Farley." The blond woman nodded at Essie and her friends.

"Did you need to ask me more questions, Detective?" asked Essie sweetly. She gave him her toothiest grin.

"Actually, Ms. Cobb, we're here to question your friend, Ms. Opal?"

"Me?" cried Opal. "What did I do?"

"Nothing, ma'am," said the female detective. "We understand that you observed the accident the other night during the fireworks display . . ."

"The accident that resulted in the injury to one of the residents here, a Mr. Lester Mills?" added the male detective, checking his notebook.

"And that put us both in the hospital," added Essie.

"Why, yes, I did," responded Opal. She looked skeptical and was pulling on her necklace with both hands, a gesture Essie knew indicated an extreme amount of nervousness on Opal's part.

"We'd like to get your description of the accident, if we could," said the man.

"Of course," agreed Opal.

"Would you prefer to go someplace more private?" asked the woman, glancing at the other three women.

"No, that's fine," said Opal. "I don't mind talking here with my friends." She smiled weakly at Essie and Marjorie. "They were there too."

"Was I ever," said Essie, pointing at the bandage on the back of her head. The detectives acknowledged her injury and moved into the circle of furniture in the corner of the lobby where the four women were seated.

They both pulled their chairs closer to Opal and opened their notebooks, poised to take down Opal's words.

"Just tell us what you remember, Ms. Opal," said the woman, gently.

"Well. . . ." began Opal, looking around, and realizing that it didn't appear that the detectives were aware of the foursome's recent excursion into the neighborhood field where they'd found potential clues. She looked at Essie as if to ask, "Should I tell them about the note and the earring and our field trip?" Essie, quickly reading Opal's worried look, gave her a brief shake of the head, trying to indicate that Opal should just give her name, rank, and serial number.

"We were all on the front yard—out there," said Opal, pointing out the glass entrance doors to the front yard where traces of the explosion could still be seen in some burnt grass. "I was sitting next to Lester—I mean, Mr. Mills—and we were having a very nice chat. . ."

"He's sweet on her," commented Marjorie.

"Marjorie!" cried Opal, "That's not true. And even if it were, it has nothing to do with what happened."

"That's fine, Ms. Opal," said Farley, her warm blue eyes shining through her glasses.

"Just go on," added Blake, all business.

"I was just talking to Mr. Mills," continued Opal. "They had just started to set off some of the fireworks over at the park and we were commenting on them and enjoying them."

"And where were you in relation to the other residents?" asked Farley, pen poised over notepad.

"We were actually sort of removed by ourselves," she said.

"So they could be alone," suggested Marjorie.

"Marjorie! Stop it!" scolded Opal. "We just happened to be sitting in seats that were apart from some of the other groupings. Fay was sitting with us."

"Fay?" asked Blake.

"Yes, our friend Fay," said Opal, indicating Fay and patting her hand. "She and I are very close and I take her with me everywhere. She doesn't speak, so I hope you weren't planning on asking her questions. . ."

"That probably won't be necessary," said Farley.

"Anyway," continued Opal, "Fay was sitting on my left and Lester was on my right. Essie came out of the building, and I saw her coming toward us, so I waved at her."

"I only came over to say hello," injected Essie. "I didn't intend to stick around and bother the lovebirds, I mean Opal and Lester . . ."

"Essie!"

"Please, go on, Ms. Opal," said Blake, obviously drowning in this sea of geriatric hormones.

"As soon as Essie came over," said Opal, "Lester immediately stood up and offered her his seat. He's very gallant."

"Yes," said Essie. "I really didn't intend to take his seat, but he was quite insistent."

"So, this Mr. Mills gave you—Ms. Essie—his seat. And then what do you remember, Ms. Opal?" urged Farley.

Opal continued: "Lester rose and was helping Essie sit down. All of a sudden, he looked up over Essie's head and his face contorted. I followed his eyes upward and saw this firecracker coming right towards him. It was awful! Lester didn't have time to move Essie so he just leaped on top of her, knocking her over backwards and away from me and Fay. The firecracker struck him and exploded. I screamed. Then everyone was yelling and running around. It was horrible!"

"Ms. Opal, this is very important. We need you to tell us as much as you can about the firecracker you saw, as it appears you were one of the few people who actually saw it hit Mr. Mills."

"As I said, it came directly at him from the west. It looked to me like what I assume a firecracker would look like, although I can't say I've seen one in ages close up. It was a long cylinder and fire was streaming from it's behind."

"What color was it?"

"I don't remember it being a specific color. Is that important?"

"I mean, was it red, white or blue?" asked Farley.

"I don't think so. It all happened so fast and the explosion was so loud and hot. I was so worried about Lester."

"And about me, I assume," added Essie.

"Yes, of course, Essie," said Opal. It was clear that having to describe what she'd witnessed that night was very difficult for Opal.

"When you first looked up in the sky where Mr. Mills was looking, what did you see?" asked Blake.

"I don't know what you mean."

"I mean," said Blake, "did you see the firecracker before you realized it was headed for Mr. Mills?"

"No, sir," replied Opal. "It was quite close when I first saw it and it was obviously headed towards Lester, or at least it was close to him."

"Can you say how far?" asked Farley.

"I don't really know how to estimate distances," sighed Opal. "Maybe at the level of the top of the building. I only saw it a second or two before it struck."

"We understand, Ms. Opal," said Farley, "and apparently, you're the only person who actually saw the firecracker strike. Everyone else we've interviewed can only tell us about the aftermath. Now that's good, but we really need to know about the firecracker itself and where it came from . . ."

"So you can catch those teenage hoodlums who probably set it off?" interrupted Essie.

"What teenage hoodlums?" asked Farley.

"I, uh, don't know," said Essie, waffling, "but I remember you told me in the hospital that Reardon has a no-fireworks policy except for in the city park, and it's illegal for individuals to set off fireworks anywhere in the city limits."

"But you don't know of any *particular* teenagers who were lighting firecrackers, do you, Miss Essie?"

"Who? Me?" she questioned. "No, of course not. I'm just repeating what you said."

Blake motioned to Farley and the two detectives rose and walked over to the front desk. The four women remained riveted in their lobby seats, glancing over to the two detectives who seemed to be having an animated discussion, possibly an argument. After a few minutes, the two officers returned to the women.

"Ladies," said Blake, "we want to thank you for allowing us to pick your brains. If you remember any more information about that night or any more information about the firecracker itself, we'd appreciate it if . . ."

"Detectives," said Essie, aloud, stopping the man's farewell speech. "Before you go, could I ask you something?"

"Of course . . ." said Blake. The two officers looked quizzically at Essie.

"I feel there's something you aren't telling us . . . about that firecracker. Maybe if you did, we might be able to help you more than we are now."

"Oh?" asked Farley, her blond hair falling, as if on cue, over her eye.

"Yes. I noticed that you seem to be fixated on Opal describing the firecracker to you. That seems a strange request for something that is, I am guessing, at best an accident by the city and, at worst, a prank gone wrong by some local hoodlums. It seems strange to me that the city would put *two* detectives on this case. Yes, a man was seriously injured, but it seems to be an accident, even if it occurred by a bunch of teenagers shooting off rockets in the field down the block . . ."

"Essie!" cried Marjorie, as soon as Essie said the word *field.*

"Possibly," agreed Blake. "We *are* interested in the firecracker."

"Now, *I* didn't see the firecracker," continued Essie, "but Opal did and if you think that having a better description of it is important, I'm certain that she'll be able to search her memory and come up with such a description. You see, Opal was an administrative assistant for a major tax firm when she was younger and details are her specialty. Maybe if you give us a *hint* as to just what you're looking for, she might be able to help you better."

"Oh, Essie, I don't know if . . ." began Opal, in response to Essie's big speech.

"All right," said Blake. He glanced at his partner, who gave him a worried look. "This is *not* for broadcasting to your fellow residents, ladies, but only for Ms. Opal's use if it might help her remember anything about the firecracker she saw. Our forensics unit has examined the remains of the firecracker and it doesn't bear any resemblance to any of those set off by the city in the park. In fact, it doesn't bear any resemblance to any *known* firecracker currently on the market."

The women all looked at him aghast and then and looked at each other.

"So you see why it's so important that we get your testimony, Ms. Opal. This firecracker, if that's truly what it is, is disintegrated. The few small pieces we have of it tell us very little about what it is or who made it or—more importantly—if it was an accident or if it was used to attack Lester Mills."

"Or—me?" asked Essie suddenly, her entire face covered in fear.

Chapter 14

Again, Essie's compatriots were struck dumb.

"Why would anyone attack you, Essie?" demanded Marjorie. "You wouldn't hurt a fly."

"I know that, Marjorie," snorted Essie, "but maybe it's some criminal who's heard about my sleuthing skills and is afraid I might ferret out his evil deeds."

"Really, Essie," snorted Opal. Fay giggled and put her hands over her face.

"Now, why does she find this so funny?" queried Essie.

"Actually, ladies," said Blake, leaning his big frame into the small group. The four women followed his lead and tightened their circle, in anticipation of some juicy police news. "We don't really *know* who *was* the target of this rocket—if anyone. All we know is that our forensics unit has discovered that it was powered by a very sophisticated guidance system—at least that's what they believe from the remains they found. This type of explosive device is a kind used presently only by the military in drone-targeted missiles."

"What!" cried Opal. "So the military is shooting at us here at Happy Haven?"

"My partner didn't say that, Miss Opal," said Farley, placing a calming hand on Opal's which were now shaking a bit. "We have no idea who set this off or how they got this weapon or why they did it. But, certainly as it was coming down, it might have resembled a regular firecracker, but it probably looked different in other respects. It's our job to find out as much as we can about the rocket and what it looked like, what any of you saw . . ."

"Yes," agreed Blake, obviously realizing that his words had greatly alarmed the four women who lived in what the four of them believed was a very safe cocoon, free from the hazards of the outside world. "We want to assure you that our military is not shooting at the residents of Happy Haven!"

"How do you know?" demanded Essie. "Did you call the Pentagon?"

"Ma'am," replied Farley, in a soft calm voice, "believe me, our superiors have reported on this to the powers that be in the military establishment. That's how our forensics unit was able to report to us about the advanced guidance system remains that were discovered on your front lawn after the rocket exploded."

"Good lord!" cried Marjorie, "This is terrifying! It's like we're in World War III!"

"Calm down, Marjorie," ordered Essie, "You're overreacting." Essie gave a stern look to her excitable friend—and also one to Opal. At the same time, she patted Fay gently on the hand that was resting on the arm of her wheelchair. "Now, Detective, you say this rocket was actually a what do you call it? A drone?"

"Yes, ma'am," replied Blake. He glanced back at Farley, uncertain if the women were stable enough to tolerate any more information about the police findings. Farley nodded at him and he began, "A drone is actually like a tiny helicopter that is controlled remotely. It has many civilian uses at the present and many more under development. The military, however, uses these drones for surveillance and often for targeting remote locations with missiles. Inexpensive drones are available for purchase by the average person to use as a hobby. Even so, civilian use is limited to flying drones for entertainment and sometimes surveillance. Civilians don't use drones for missile attacks."

"Until now," said Essie. "That's what you're saying, isn't it, Detective? That someone got a hold of one of these military drones and used it to shoot at us here at Happy Haven?"

"Yes and no," replied Farley, her warm voice taking the edge off of the rather grim details that Blake had been describing. "First of all, we doubt that any civilian could *get a hold of* an actual military drone with missile targeting capabilities, which are, by the way, much larger than what was apparently used in this situation. Second, we doubt any civilian, even if they could get an appropriate drone, would be able to find a compatible missile—and military missiles have a huge explosive capability. The explosion that injured Mr. Mills was relatively small. Third, assuming that someone even had the drone and a usable missile, *why* would they want to target a senior retirement community?"

"Or one of its residents?" asked Essie, pointing at herself. "I've heard, detective, that these drones are quite sophisticated and accurate in their targeting. I believe I read that a drone missile can target a lone person from miles away."

"Yes," agreed Blake, checking his notebook, where he evidently had information stored from the forensics unit, "A drone can be programmed to hone in on a specific target, lock onto it, and then shoot a missile at the target with virtually 100 percent accuracy."

"So, if they were targeting me," continued Essie, "they reached their target and the only reason I'm alive is because some man jumped on me right before it struck. Do you think that somebody wants me dead?"

"Essie," said Opal, "who in the world would want you dead?"

"I don't have the foggiest. It could be anyone. Picky sticky! You know I annoy everyone," she said, stamping her feet.

"That's true," said Marjorie, out of the side of her mouth, then gave Essie a giant smile.

"Ma'am," interrupted Blake. The four women were getting worked up wondering who was planning to do away with their leader. "Ma'am, Ms. Cobb, before you get too concerned, I should point out to you that *you* were not originally sitting in that chair on the night of the Fourth. Mr. Mills had been sitting there most of the evening. He only relinquished his seat to you so that you could sit beside your friend here. A gentlemanly thing to do. If he hadn't done that, the rocket would have struck him in the back of the head, instead of the backside and he would, no doubt, be dead now."

"So, detective," said Essie, catching on, "you're saying that if this rocket *was* shot off by a drone, it was probably aimed at Mr. Mills?"

"It's really the more likely scenario," agreed Blake. Farley nodded her head.

"So Lester's gallantry may have saved his own life?" questioned Opal, hand to her throat.

"Possibly. We surmise that if he'd remained seated and the rocket had struck where it actually did, it would have hit him in the back of the head, just as it would have hit you in the back of the head, Ms. Cobb, if Mr. Mills hadn't knocked you over backwards. Truly, his actions to protect you not only saved your life, but saved his own as well."

"Wait a minute," said Essie, holding up a hand. "You said whoever set this drone to fire this rocket wasn't a military person?"

"We're not sure, but we don't think so," replied Farley.

"So how did they, you know, target Mr. Mills, when he was just sitting there on the front lawn? Do they have some headquarters somewhere to view Happy Haven from the sky? I mean, how did they do this?"

"Well . . ." said Blake with a big sigh.

"You don't know, do you?" demanded Essie.

"No, ma'am," said Blake, shaking his head. "Most of these recreational drones just allow the operator to fly the drone and then land it. They really don't have the capability that the military does to target specific locations and fire rockets. But our forensics unit is working on it." He smiled brightly and Farley joined him.

"Poppycock!" cried Essie. "You people don't have a clue what you're doing. I know it."

"Essie!" cried Opal.

"Essie, that's no way to act," agreed Marjorie. "The police are trying to help us find out who did this—who harmed Lester and you."

"I assure you, Ms. Cobb," began Blake.

"Ms. Cobb," started Farley to assist her partner, but Essie was having none of it.

"If all you say is true, detectives," said Essie, standing up, "and this rocket is apparently some super-sophisticated drone-operated missile that only the military uses, then you tell me why some average citizen would have one of these, and more importantly, why they would shoot it at Happy Haven and—even more more importantly—since these things can be targeted so precisely, why would they target me? Or Mr. Mills? Because it seems to me that somebody has it in for one of the two of us, and *that* had better be your major concern now—not asking Opal to describe what the darn thing looked like as it rained death down on all of us the other night!"

With that, Essie grabbed her walker and manipulated it with great precision (probably just like a drone-operated missile) around the knees of all the people who were sitting in the little group and stormed out of the lobby and down the hallway to her room.

"Should we go after her?" asked Farley to the remaining women.

"Oh, no," replied Marjorie, brightly. "She gets like that. She's feisty. You know. She'll probably solve the crime for you though. If you don't want her to beat you to the punch, you'd better get hopping." Marjorie shot the detectives her warmest smile.

"Marjorie," said Opal, giving her pal a scowl. "That's not polite. We're sorry, detectives, for our friend's behavior. Of course, we want to help you in any way we can. I promise you I will try to remember anything I can about the firecracker as it was coming down."

"That would be most helpful, ma'am," said Blake. "And, uh, what about your friend?" He gestured to Fay. "You said she was there with you? Did she see the rocket too?"

"Well, I'm sure she did, Detective," answered Opal, "but Fay is mute. She can't speak."

"Does she understand?" asked Farley, as Blake was apparently ready to leave.

"Oh, yes," said Opal. "Before she came here, Fay was a librarian, so we know she spoke at one time. But she's all alone here; she has no family. Her pension covers her bills, so nobody here really knows when or why she became mute. We believe something happened to her late in her life but before she arrived here at Happy Haven that caused her to quit speaking. Oh, I know! She does use the computer. Actually, she's very good at it."

"Can she write? I mean, can she type?" asked Blake.

"I don't know," replied Opal. "She's never typed any messages since I've known her, and I've been here since she arrived, which was at least eight years ago. When she arrived we just sort of . . . bonded, and I've been her companion ever since. I take her around places, although she is capable of maneuvering her wheelchair herself, but it's difficult for her."

Farley opened her notebook up to a blank page and handed the notebook and a short pencil to Fay. Fay was somewhat surprised when given the items but she took them and smiled at the lady policeman.

"Ms. Fay," said Farley, pulling her chair closer to Fay's wheelchair and leaning in, "we're very interested in the firecracker that hit Mr. Mills the other evening. Did you see it? Can you tell us anything about it?"

Fay held onto the notebook and the pencil and looked at each item in turn. She turned the pencil over and over between her fingers.

"This isn't going to work, Farley," whispered Blake.

"She's mute, Blake, not deaf," replied Farley, scowling at her partner and then smiling at Fay. She gestured to Fay to write in the notebook.

Fay lowered her head to the notepad and slowly began to rub the pencil back and forth and roll the tip around and around.

"She's just making a mess," announced Blake.

"Quiet!" reprimanded his partner, her hand held up, her attention now totally on the little lady in the wheelchair.

Fay continued to scribble on the notepad for several minutes. She had the little book tilted in such a way that none of the people sitting around her could see what she was drawing. Finally, when she was finished, she handed the pencil back to Farley and turned the notebook around and held her picture up so that everyone could see it. The drawing was clearly one of the firecracker. It showed a long, cylindrical shape with sparks jetting from the rear. The cylinder was sub-divided into three equal parts with the top part coming to a point and with each part slightly smaller in circumference than the one below it. The bottom portion from which the sparks emitted was the largest of the three segments. On the middle segment, Fay had written some letters and numbers—ME85.

"Wow!" declared Blake as he beheld the precise drawing.

"Ms. Fay," asked Farley carefully, "is this the firecracker you saw that hit Mr. Mills the other night?" Fay nodded twice.

Chapter 15

Essie had not gone directly back to her room. Half way down her hallway, she turned her walker around and quietly pushed it back to the entrance of the lobby where she stood discreetly watching the scene as Fay drew the picture of the rocket. Essie was immediately aware of what Fay was doing and the fact that their silent little companion was probably an ideal eye witness. She was also aware that she wasn't the only one watching the detectives interrogating Fay. Across the lobby, standing at the entrance to the back of the kitchen where the mailboxes were, was their manager, Felix Federico. He was staring at the group surrounding Fay with a strangely worried look on his otherwise cheerful face.

As Essie continued to watch, the detectives stood up and began to leave. The young female detective placed the drawing that Fay had made inside her notebook, and then placed the notebook inside her jacket pocket. She bent down and took Fay's hand, obviously thanking her for her input. The man, Blake, gestured to his partner, and the two of them headed out the entrance. Essie noted that with the departure of the detectives, Felix Federico turned from his position near the mailboxes and headed down the hallway into the main offices across from the front desk. Essie's pals were still congregated around Fay. Marjorie and Opal were seated and both of them were chatting together and leaning in to Fay, touching her shoulder and patting her hand. Fay was smiling happily in response to their attention.

Essie used this opportunity to sneak around behind them and down a hallway off the other side of the lobby to the various activity rooms. Here she quickly entered a small room that contained several desks that were set up with computers. Essie frequently used these computers to do research that aided her in her sleuthing. It had been difficult at first, but now she was a whiz at searching the Internet and doing keyword searches. She shoved her walker over to one of the desks. Luckily, the room was totally empty this late in the afternoon; probably most of the residents were getting ready for dinner.

Her fingers flashing, Essie started her search. She entered all sorts of terms in the search box in an attempt to learn everything she could about drones and missiles and rockets and firecrackers—and how, if at all, they were related. She discovered that the use of drones was becoming extremely popular, with military and civilian uses burgeoning by leaps and bounds. The military, she learned, was already using drones for reconnaissance as well as actual weaponry. Civilian use held even more potential, with prognosticators envisioning drones being used in weather prediction, law enforcement, and even package delivery. She was surprised to learn that anyone could now purchase his or her own recreational drone online to use for fun. She investigated these types of drones, wondering if it was possible for one of her enemies to transform one of these toy drones into a potential killing machine that had dropped from the sky on Lester Mills the other night. She realized that anyone who might do such a thing would have to have a great deal of technical knowledge, and she didn't know anyone who might dislike her so much that they'd want to go to all that trouble to do her in.

Rabble dabble, she thought, *I may annoy some people here at Happy Haven, but I don't think I make anyone mad enough to want to kill me, and surely not to put in this type of effort.*

The more she thought about it, the more she thought that the intended victim of the rocket strike must have been Lester Mills—if it was any particular person at all. It might have been someone who just hated Happy Haven, she surmised. Maybe it was the child or relative of a resident who felt his or her loved one had been mistreated and wanted to punish Happy Haven. That seemed like an awfully strange and awkward way to do it though. Yet, the very fact that the detectives had indicated that the remains of the rocket were not your typical firecracker seemed to indicate something more sinister—not just some hoodlums shooting off firecrackers, but someone targeting Happy Haven, whoever that someone might be. But how did they do it? Was it one of these toy drones that anyone could buy online and someone bought one of those and then outfitted it with a firecracker? That seemed so unlikely. Who could do that? And if they could, why would they want to? *Oh, I'm just going in circles,* thought Essie to herself.

She reached in her pocket and brought out the *clues* that she and Marjorie had found out in the field earlier that day. She stared at the piece of paper with the math homework on it—or at least that's what it looked like. Attempting to read some of the strange symbols and numbers on the paper, she tried to enter some of the jargon into the search box on the computer. *This will probably never work,* she thought. She hit the *enter* key. The monitor lit up with a list of articles. Essie read titles that included words such as *modeling, unmanned, aerial, vehicle, uav, flight trajectory, quad rotor* and more. *Oh, Jane's brains!* she exclaimed to herself. *This isn't some young fellow's homework. This is something that the perpetrator of the crime dropped.* Indeed, the paper contained formulas and numbers that Essie realized must be related to the rocket that had struck Lester Mills. She examined the piece of paper more closely. It didn't appear to be anything important— more like a snippet of scratch paper that someone had jotted down a few ideas on, and then either dropped accidentally or even just tossed away because it was of no use anymore. This piece of paper certainly did seem to indicate that Essie and Marjorie had located the spot from where the rocket had been launched.

"That's where we found the earring too!" she said out loud, placing the gold dangly piece of jewelry on the computer table as she examined it more closely. Now that she had time to look at the earring more carefully, she could see that Marjorie was right, and that it was not just some ordinary piece of costume jewelry. It was real gold—at least to Essie's untrained eye. The dangly part encased one red stone which certainly looked like a ruby. That was then surrounded by at least a dozen small diamonds. And if it *was* real, it was probably a very expensive earring. Certainly whoever dropped it would be looking for it—not only because it was worth a lot of money, but also potentially because it was dropped at what Essie now realized was a crime scene.

She contemplated searching for information about the earring or the ruby and the diamonds in it on the Internet, but couldn't think of any term to search. She leaned back in the rolling computer desk chair and folded her arms.

What should I do? she wondered. *Obviously, these items are important clues, but if I go to the police, I'll have to tell them that Marjorie and I went snooping around out in that field. I've already been scolded for sneaking out of my hospital bed to visit Lester in the middle of the night. Every time I turn around, somebody is shaking a finger at me.*

Essie placed her head on the computer desk, trying to think what to do.

All of a sudden, Marjorie walked in.

"Essie!" she called out. "There you are! We've been looking all over for you. You weren't in your room after the detectives left, and we were worried about you."

"Oh, Marjorie," said Essie, looking up. She quickly slid the note and the earring back into her pocket, smiling and scooting her chair out from the desk.

"What are you doing here?" asked Marjorie. "We're ready to go to dinner. Are you coming with us?"

"I . . .I . . ."

"Oh, Essie, you shouldn't have left when you did," said Marjorie, coming to stand by Essie. "Fay remembered what the rocket looked like that hit you and Lester. She drew a perfect picture of it for the detectives! I think they were extremely pleased. Looks like Fay may turn out to be as great a detective as you, Essie." Marjorie gave Essie a knowing little grin.

"That's nice," said Essie in a distracted manner.

"You're not jealous?" asked Marjorie, waiting for Essie to gather her belongings and her walker.

"Of course not," replied Essie, pushing her walker out the door, Marjorie following behind. "I think we should talk about all of this."

"We will, Essie," said Marjorie, nodding.

"We have a lot to cover," said Essie. She shoved her walker down the hallway. "But, you go on to dinner. I need to visit the potty first." She swerved suddenly to the left and headed down the hallway to her apartment. Marjorie stood in the lobby tapping her foot. She glanced over at the dining room. She could see Opal and Fay now being seated at their regular table through the glass walls. After a few minutes, Marjorie looked back down Essie's hallway to see the little silver-haired dynamo storming back.

"What are you waiting for?" demanded Essie, rolling past Marjorie and into the dining hall. She rolled over to their regular table and plopped down in her regular chair across from Fay. Marjorie followed her and also seated herself. Immediately, Santos was there, filling their water glasses.

"Coffee, ladies?" he asked.

"Iced tea for me, Santos," said Marjorie.

"Me too," agreed Essie.

"*And* me," added Opal. She looked at Fay, who glanced around smiling. "I'm guessing Fay will want tea too. Fay! Tea?" Fay looked over at Opal and smiled. "Tea, Fay?" Opal asked again and Fay continued to smile. "Get her tea, Santos," said Opal. "Really, Fay, "you can draw a picture of an aerial drone missile when asked to by the local constabulary, but you can't let us know if you want coffee or tea."

"Opal," chastised Marjorie, "That's not like you. You're always so patient with Fay."

"Don't worry, Marjorie," cajoled Essie, "If Fay doesn't drink her tea, we can order her coffee. I'm sure they have plenty in the kitchen. Now, down to work."

"Down to work?" asked Opal. "It's supper time, Essie. Haven't we done enough for one day? I mean traipsing around the neighborhood, then that interrogation with the police . . ."

"Traipsing, Opal?" declared Marjorie. "I was the one doing the traipsing. You and Fay just stood around on the sidewalk. And Fay did all the work for the detective. You just sat there."

"Ladies!" cried Essie, as Santos brought their beverages. "We have a lot to discuss. Let's not spend our meal time arguing."

"Have you ladies decided yet?" asked Santos, pen poised in hand over his notepad.

"Oh, heavens!" cried Opal, "I'm so hungry from this exhausting day." She glanced down at the menu in front of her. "Ooo! Spaghetti and meat balls. I'll have that." She beamed, suddenly forgetting her state of exhaustion.

"Me too," added Marjorie.

"Me three," said Essie.

"And Miss Fay?" asked Santos, waiting for Opal to order for her friend as usual.

"Her four," said Opal. "And if she doesn't like it, she can draw you a picture of what she wants." The women, excluding Fay, who looked around bewildered, all laughed heartily.

Chapter 16

The four pals all enjoyed their dinner of juicy, spicy spaghetti and meat balls—one of their favorites. Afterwards, while they were sipping their iced tea and relaxing, the conversation moved back to the recent excitement on the Fourth of July.

"Essie," said Marjorie, "We have to talk about what we found in the field."

"You mean that paper and that earring?" asked Opal.

"Yes," replied Essie, reaching into the pocket of her trousers and bringing out the folded up piece of paper and the gold earring. She placed the two objects in the center of the table. "We found these close together in a small clearing. I don't think the police had been there."

Opal picked up the piece of paper and unfolded it. She peered at it, dropping her glasses a bit in an attempt to decipher the symbols. "It's a lot of gibberish."

"It looks like some teenager's math homework to me," added Marjorie. "That's what I told Essie. I'm guessing it belongs to the boy who set off the rocket. He should have stayed home and worked on his homework."

"That's where you're both wrong," announced Essie brightly.

"Now how would you know, Essie?" asked Marjorie. "You don't know anything about math."

"No, that's true," agreed Essie, "but I do know how to use a computer and how to conduct an Internet search, which I did just a little bit ago while you were all sitting there in the lobby gushing over those two detectives!"

"Oh, really?" asked Opal, sitting up to her full height, which was very tall. "I believe our time was well spent with the detectives as Fay was able to identify the rocket. Truly, more than identify. She was able to produce an exact image of that rocket that rained down death upon Lester. Surely that's worth more than you scrounging around out in that old field looking for junk."

"Yes, Essie, Fay drew them a picture of the rocket," announced Marjorie, proud of her friend, patting Fay on her shoulder.

"A very detailed one too," added Opal. "I was standing right there with her when that rocket came down and I don't remember the details Fay remembered that the rocket had three segments and the middle segment had letters and numbers on it."

"What letters and numbers?" asked Essie.

"I don't remember exactly, do you, Marjorie?" asked Opal, turning to her friend.

"The letters were *M-E* with some numbers. I don't remember which numbers," replied Marjorie.

"Anyway," continued Opal, "I'm sure what Fay did for the detectives will help them a lot more than your little foray into the field and whatever clues you found. I mean—a piece of paper and some old costume jewelry. Junk!"

"This is not junk, Opal," replied Essie, shaking her shoulders. "See those markings there." She pointed out formulas on the paper, shoving the note right up close to Opal's eyes. "This is not some kid's homework. This is a secret formula for the drone that struck us."

"What?" cried Opal and Marjorie together. "Are you crazy, Essie?" added Opal.

"No, I'm not crazy, Opal," snorted Essie. "I typed this formula here into the search engine on the computer and up popped all sorts of articles on drones and rockets and missiles and things like that. I'm sure our culprit is the one who dropped this paper; it ties him directly to the rocket."

"Well, if that's so," argued Marjorie, "then why didn't you give it to the detectives?" She gave Essie a sweet smile, as no one wanted to get on Essie's bad side when she was in a fury as she was now.

"Marjorie," said Essie, "I just found this information out in the computer room. How could I tell the detectives? They'd already left."

"Lucky for you," mumbled Opal, behind her napkin.

"But you had the paper and the earring with you when the detectives were here," argued Marjorie. "Why didn't you show them what you had then?"

"Marjorie," said Essie, with a sigh, sipping her tea, "Then I didn't know for sure that these two clues were connected to the rocket. You said yourself that the paper was probably some kid's homework. And why would anyone drop an earring like this?"

"Like what?" asked Opal. "Are we dealing with a cross-dressing bomber?"

"I don't know!" cried Essie, "but look at it." She picked up the earring and held it up for the other three women to see. "Does this earring look like cheap costume jewelry? Like something some high school girl—or boy—would wear?"

"I tell you, it's real," said Marjorie.

Opal changed her demeanor as she gently took the earring from Essie and began to examine it. "Hmm," she said softly. "You're right. This is real gold, I'm sure. And, Good Lord, I think this could be a real ruby."

"Do you know how much a real ruby of this size would be worth?" asked Marjorie.

Opal continued to clutch the earring firmly in her palm and looked around the entire dining room to see if anyone had possibly been listening in.

"I don't know, but if it *is* real," said Opal firmly, "then we *must* take theses clues to Detective Blake and Detective Farley. They told us to contact them if we had anything important to add. These two clues are certainly important."

"But we'll have to admit to them that we were rummaging around out in the field," said Essie.

"So we all bite the bullet; it's for a good cause," added Marjorie. "Come on, Essie. Our embarrassment is little to pay if what we found will help solve this mystery and find the person who hurt Lester. Someone is out there who did this and we can help the police find that person."

"You have to do it, Essie," urged Opal. "Think of poor Lester, lying there in the hospital."

"I am thinking of him," said Essie. "*He* was the victim of this attack. *He* was the intended target . . ."

"Intended target?" said Opal. "What do you mean, *intended* target? Surely, you don't think someone was *intentionally* trying to hurt Lester?"

"I do, Opal," responded Essie. "Why do you think they used a drone? Just what *is* a drone? Why does the military use drones in the first place? I'll tell you. So they can target things from a *distance*. So they can target a bad guy from a distance and then drop a missile on his head without having to engage said bad guy in hand-to-hand combat. Just think. It saves the military a lot in money and lives. You've seen those films on television where they show a target and then all of a sudden—boom!—an explosion and they announce that so-and-so bad guy was blown up by one of these things—and no American soldiers were hurt. It's fantastic, that is, until you're the one in the sights of one of these drone things."

"You're being ridiculous, Essie," said Opal. "No one targeted Lester with a drone. Who would do such a thing? I mean no one would go that far."

"Maybe not," agreed Essie, "but we don't know for sure. I mean, he's a brand new resident. What do we know about him? Only what *you've* told us, Opal, and you haven't seen him in years. Who knows what sort of trouble he may have gotten into in the intervening time. Who knows? He could have become a spy and some agent from another country could be trying to wipe him out."

"That's ridiculous," laughed Marjorie. "All I have to do is think about him dancing to *Uptown Funk* the other night and I realize he doesn't threaten anyone."

"Well, if they weren't targeting Lester, I still say it *could* be me," said Essie, not really willing to relinquish her position as the most likely person to be offed by the mysterious enemy.

"You sound like you *want* it to be you," declared Marjorie.

"Of course not," said Essie, "but I am unique and some people just don't like it when someone else stands out from the crowd." Essie gave her tablemates her most haughty look.

"Be that as it may, Essie," said Opal, "if you refuse to take these clues to the detectives, then I think we should at least function on the theory that Lester is the most likely target and do whatever we can to protect him."

"I agree with Opal," said Marjorie.

"Oh, all right," said Essie.

"And going along with that theory," continued Opal, "I believe we need to focus our attention on him."

"Okay, Opal," said Essie, "then you'd better enlighten us all with everything you know about this man. And I don't mean how gallant he was when he came to visit the tax firm where you worked, or how courteous he was to his wife, or anything like that. We'll have to dig *much* deeper."

"I agree," said Opal. This shocked Essie.

"Oh, well, good then," said Essie.

"And along those lines, let me provide you all with some basic background on Lester Mills," said Opal, reaching into her large purse and pulling out several sheets of typed paper. "I took it upon myself to type up some information about Lester. Here is biographical information. Background on his company and his family. His ancestors, his holdings, his finances, basically anything I could find."

"When did you do all this, Opal?" asked Essie.

"Last night in the computer room," replied Opal. "I suspected we might need to know more about Lester's background, and you're not the only one who can handle a mouse, Essie. I simply didn't have time to distribute the information to you all today what with the trip to the field and then the interrogation by the detectives. But now that you have this information, we can go over it, and if any of you see anything you want to discuss or ask, we can do so."

The women each thumbed through the three-page synopsis stapled together at the top corner that Opal had provided for all. Even Fay had her own copy. She held it sideways and flipped the paper up and down like a multi-page fan.

"This is a waste of effort on Fay," said Marjorie, looking over at their wheelchair-bound buddy.

"Possibly," said Opal, "but I always like to include her in our group."

The women were quiet for a while as they perused the single-spaced story of the life of Lester Mills.

"He's an engineer," said Essie. "That uses a lot of math."

"Indeed it does," agreed Opal. "You will note that he formed his own company—Mills Electronics—when he was very young and it still flourishes today."

"His wife was from a rich family in New York," added Marjorie. "You even have her photograph here. She was quite beautiful. And evidently much younger. There was a good twenty years difference in their ages."

"I remember her well," said Opal. "As I've mentioned before, they were devoted to each other. He really seemed lost without her after she passed away. They had three children—James, Joseph, and Julie. I don't think they're very far apart in age."

"I guess the important question that I really wasn't able to answer on my handout here, is did or does Lester Mills have any enemies? I certainly wasn't able to find any indication in any of the online material that there were any, but I hope if we all put on our thinking caps . . ."

"Our thinking caps, Opal?" chided Marjorie.

"Yes, Marjorie," replied Opal, slightly unnerved, "I'm worried about my . . . friend Lester. He's lying unconscious in a hospital and it's beginning to look quite possible that this was not an accident and that someone tried to kill him."

"Maybe," said Marjorie.

Essie thought back to her night in the hospital and her visit to the unconscious Lester Mills. *The man and woman who had entered his room in the middle of the night and then abruptly left. Were they two of Mills' children? Or business rivals? And why were they there? Surely, his children had a logical reason to be at their father's bedside, but then why would they leave so suddenly when they saw Essie sitting there?* She continued to think about this strange episode as she read over the material Opal had found on Lester Mills.

"Marjorie," said Essie suddenly, "would you mind waiting here with Fay while Opal and I go somewhere?"

"Where?" asked Marjorie.

"Just to my room for a second," replied Essie.

"Oh, all right," said Marjorie, shrugging her shoulders. "It's you and me, Fay."

Essie motioned to Opal and the two women headed out of the dining room.

Chapter 17

Essie pushed her walker pell-mell through the lobby and down her hallway with Opal close behind.

"Good gracious, Essie," cried Opal. "What's the big rush? Where did you learn to pilot that thing so fast?"

"I just hang on, Opal, and my trusty walker leads the way!" cried Essie, like a train conductor. "Here we are! All passengers off!" Essie rolled quickly to her door and giving it a little bump with the front of her walker, pushed it open and stormed through into her living room. Opal followed. Essie turned and shut the door as Opal headed over to the couch and sat down, breathing deeply.

"That was exercise, Essie," she said, leaning back into the cushions, panting.

"Listen, Opal," said Essie, plopping down in her rocker and getting right to business. "It's obvious that something fishy is going on—and Lester Mills is at the heart of it,"

"It does seem that way," sighed Opal, drawing an embroidered hanky from the side of her sleeve of her pink sweater and patting her eyes.

"Now don't go getting all teary-eyed on me, Opal," admonished Essie. She glared at her friend. "Your friend is stuck over there in the hospital in a coma,"

"I know that, Essie," sobbed Opal. "It's terrible. I barely get to say hello to him and he's taken from me." Opal suddenly lost her prim and proper demeanor and began to wail.

"Wiggling piglets!" declared Essie, "Stop that! How can we help him if you're going to turn all mushy on me? I need you in top form with all of your administrative and secretarial skills intact if we're going to figure this out and prevent whoever attacked Mr. Mills with that rocket from trying again."

"Trying again?" gasped Opal. "Do you think they would?"

"Opal, if someone was actually targeting your boyfriend on the evening of the Fourth, well, they know they didn't succeed. It's been in the newspapers. They also probably know that he's now lying in a hospital bed which makes him a perfect target. If they really want him dead, don't you think they'll probably try again?"

"Essie, I just can't follow where your brain goes half the time," said Opal, shaking her head. "You're telling me you think that Lester is still in danger? That whoever shot him with that rocket is still trying to kill him?"

"That's exactly what I think, Opal," stated Essie. "This information you typed up for us on Mr. Mills and his company is a good starting place, but this is information anyone could find if they went searching for it, right?"

"Well, yes," admitted Opal. She sniffed back another tear.

"Opal, we need much more pertinent information. Information on who would have a grudge against Lester Mills and why. Your research tells us how successful he is—or was—and how wealthy, but it doesn't give any reasons *why* anyone would want to harm him. Does he have any business enemies? What about family? Does he get along with his children? I've seen them here at Happy Haven with him. I even think I may have seen two of them in his hospital room when I was there . . ."

"When you just *happened* to be in his room . . ."

"Maybe I planned it," said Essie, sheepishly, "but I really just wanted to see if he was okay. After all, the man did save my life. Can't I be grateful?"

"In my experience with you, Essie," said Opal smugly, "you always have an ulterior motive."

"Opal!" cried Essie, "how could you? I'm just a sweet little old grandma." She gave Opal her cheesiest smile and put her thumbs in her ears and waggled her fingers to punctuate her sarcasm. "Anyway, I want to discuss the reason I dragged you to my room."

"Yes," said Opal, "what's so secretive that you can't tell Marjorie or Fay?"

"Oh, we'll tell them," said Essie, "just not in the dining hall. That place has ears and I don't want anyone to know our plans."

"What plans?" asked Opal.

"We're going to break into Lester's room," announced Essie.

"What? Why?" cried Opal.

"*What* is just what I said—the four of us are going to break into Lester's room," repeated Essie. "It's not something we haven't done before. Don't you remember when . . ."

"Yes, yes, yes," said Opal, "but I'd rather forget that. Essie, we can't break in. As Lester is in the hospital, I'm sure management has locked his room, even if he did leave it unlocked. How do you plan to get in? And why would you?"

"I've already solved that problem," whispered Essie, leaning forward in her rocker. "While Phyllis was turned away talking to someone on the phone, I bent over the front desk and grabbed her master key." Essie reached into the pocket of her trousers and brought out a large gold key tied to a small placard. She waved it in the air as she watched Opal's eyes grow wide.

"No!" cried Opal. "You didn't!"

"I did!" replied Essie. "Now you see why I didn't want to discuss this in the dining room and why we need to do it now—so I can return the key before Phyllis becomes suspicious."

"Oh, Essie!" moaned Opal, head in her hands, "what are we going to do with you?"

"Do with me?" cried Essie. "There's nothing to do with me, Opal. I'm going to solve this mystery, or rather this *crime*. And I'm going to solve it before Lester Mills is attacked again."

"What do you mean attacked *again*?"

"Opal, as I said before, when I was visiting your boyfriend in the hospital in the middle of the night, he had *other* visitors. One of his sons and his daughter—or at least, I think that's who they were—came sneaking into his room around two in the morning. When they saw me they snuck right back out."

"So?" said Opal, her face and body a mass of incredulity.

"So, you don't find that a little odd?"

"Odd that a man's children would want to visit him in the hospital?" demanded Opal. "No, Essie. Not at all."

"But, in the middle of the night? And secretively. They never informed the floor nurse that they were there. And, when they saw me sitting there, they rushed back out. Don't you think that if they were just visiting, they would have stayed and asked who I was and, well, oh, I don't know, Opal. It was just creepy." She pushed herself out of her chair and grabbed her walker and stormed back and forth in front of her window. "You think I'm being too impulsive?"

Opal sat there staring at Essie, contemplating everything her friend had just told her.

"You say they sneaked in?" asked Opal. "What do you mean?"

"I mean that they were extremely quiet when they entered. They didn't say, 'Hi, Dad!' or 'How are you, Dad?' or anything like that. I don't know who she thought I was—maybe a nurse, but she certainly wasn't expecting to see anyone sitting there in her father's room by his bedside."

"They might have just been quiet because they didn't want to wake him . . ."

"He's in a coma," cried Essie. "I hardly think that's an issue."

"I don't know, Essie. It seems really far-fetched."

"But you're considering it, aren't you?" Essie asked, pushing her walker back to Opal.

"Just say that you might be correct . . ."

"I am," said Essie.

"If you were," suggested Opal, "then what is it you want to find or expect to find by searching Lester's apartment?"

"I don't know," said Essie, a demoralized tone invading her voice as she plopped back down in her rocking chair. "You remember the last time we searched an apartment. We didn't know what we'd find then but we searched anyway and we found gold. Well, not real gold, but a great clue."

"True," agreed Opal. "I guess we could try. But we'd have to have Marjorie and Fay help us."

"I agree," said Essie. "You and Fay can serve as look-outs in the hallway just in case anyone from management comes by. Marjorie and I will do the searching."

There was a knock on Essie's door.

"Oh, no!" Essie said, pushing herself from her chair and going to answer the door. Marjorie was standing there, hand poised to knock again.

"Gracious, Marjorie!" cried Opal. "You're supposed to be with Fay. You didn't leave her alone, did you?"

"No, of course not," replied Marjorie, entering the apartment and shutting the door behind her. "I know you two are up to no good, so spit it out. What's going on?"

"Who's watching Fay?" demanded Opal. "You can't leave her with just anybody."

"I left her with the manager," declared Marjorie, pushing her way into Essie's living room and depositing her handbag on Essie's coffee table.

"You mean Felix?" asked Opal. "He won't know what to do?"

"What are you talking about, Opal? He manages a retirement home. Of course, he'll know what to do," said Essie.

"And he adores Fay," replied Marjorie. "He gushes over her more than he does any of us. He was thrilled when I asked if he'd watch her for a few minutes while I went to track you down, Opal. Remember, you're her companion and you're the one who's expected to get her to and from her room. You took on that chore willingly, if I remember correctly."

"Of course I did," answered Opal, "and I never leave her alone when we're out and about—except for now. Essie, you see the problems you cause." She turned to Essie and shook her finger at her.

"Me?" cried Essie. "Marjorie deserted her, not me."

"Oh, for heaven's sake!" cried Marjorie. "Just tell me what's going on and then we can all go back and get Fay."

Essie sighed and quickly filled Marjorie in on her plans to search Lester Mills' room. Unlike Opal, Marjorie was immediately on board. She was definitely the more adventurous of the two, observed Essie. With a quick description of everyone's duties, the trio took off to get Fay and start their snooping.

They entered the dining room and were immediately relieved to see that Fay was still there at their table and still safe. Felix Federico was sitting beside her, holding her hand. The duo had their heads very close together and Felix was speaking to Fay very softly. Fay was looking into Felix's eyes, glued to his every word. It seemed quite obvious that Fay enjoyed his words. Felix seemed so wrapped up in his discussion with Fay that he was totally oblivious to the presence of the other three women, now the only people remaining in the dining room.

Essie, Opal, and Marjorie moved closer to their table slowly, unable or unwilling to interrupt the *conversation* that was taking place between their friend Fay and the retirement center's head man. When they were within a few feet, they could hear Felix's words.

" . . . lovely lady. I remember well. You have such a beautiful smile just like . . . ." He held her hand in his left hand as he gently caressed it with his right hand.

"Fay!" said Opal, as the three women approached the table. "Sorry we deserted you."

"Oh, ladies!" replied Felix, looking up at them while still holding onto Fay's hands. "It is no problem. Fay and I, we are simpatico."

"Yes, we see that—very simpatico, whatever that is," said Essie, giving him a short smile and motioning for Opal to take over Fay's wheelchair, which she did.

"Oh, Felix!" cried Marjorie, distracting him as the other two whisked Fay away. "Sorry, we need Fay. For, for . . . an errand. Bye!" She gave the man a flirty little shake of her hips and then quickly followed her pals out of the dining hall. Felix sat dumbfounded as the four ladies scurried out of the dining hall.

Chapter 18

"Let's go!" said Essie, leading the group towards the elevator. She glanced over her shoulder as they passed through the lobby to see if Phyllis had perchance noticed her missing master key. The receptionist was talking casually on the phone with a warm smile on her face. Essie breathed a deep sigh of relief. Essie pressed the elevator button when Opal rounded the lobby corner pushing Fay in her wheelchair. The elevator arrived almost immediately—after all, it only had one floor to go to.

The women hurried into the empty chamber and Essie pushed the button for the second floor. After the door closed, everyone but Fay started talking at once. "What's the plan?" "Just do what I tell you!" and "What's going on?" Fay looked back and forth from face to face as everyone talked at once.

"Quiet!" demanded Essie, finally, as the elevator door opened. She rolled her walker out and into the second floor lobby. "Opal, you and Fay stay here. If anyone gets off the elevator who looks suspicious, come down to Lester's room right away and get us out!"

"Essie," countered Opal, "how am I supposed to do that pushing Fay? You know she slows me down."

"You're right," agreed Essie. "I know, we all go to Lester's room first and once we see where it is, then Opal and Fay, you go stand at the closest hall intersection and if you see anyone coming who looks suspicious, just leave Fay there for a second, come get us out fast and we'll all run back, grab Fay, and run the other way. Now, let's go. I can't keep this master key all day."

"Essie," asked Marjorie, "do you even know what room is Lester's?"

"Of course, I do," replied Essie, "I checked on that earlier too. He's in 29B."

"So we need to go down this hallway," said Opal, pointing the opposite direction from where they were headed."

"Right," said Essie, making a sudden full turn with her walker and barreling down a long hallway to the left of the elevator. The other two women followed, Opal pushing Fay's wheelchair at a decidedly slower pace.

Essie pointed to the room numbers on the doors as she went—15B, 16B, 17B, 18B, 19B. They arrived at a dead end where the hallway split. Rooms 20B-25B were to the left and 26B-30B were to the right.

"Opal," said Essie, "you and Fay stay here. Lester's room must be just a few doors down." The women looked down the hallway and could see the end which was marked by a table with a flower arrangement and a mirror above it. "Keep your eyes pealed for anyone getting off the elevator. If you see Lester's children, or the detectives, or management, or anyone who might cause us a problem, come straight to Lester's room and knock. Marjorie and I will leave immediately."

"You mean, just leave Fay here?" asked Opal.

"Just long enough to come knock on Lester's door," said Essie. "Then go right back to her and get the heck out of Dodge."

"You mean walk past whoever it is you're trying to avoid?"

"Opal," argued Essie, her patience now shot, "you and Fay aren't the ones in the man's room illegally.

You're just walking around on the second floor, which you are totally free to do here. Just do it."

Essie turned and started down the left-hand hallway with Marjorie close behind. Opal and Fay did as Essie demanded and remained at the hallway intersection in case anyone got off the elevator.

Essie looked back and forth from one side of the hallway to the other. The room numbers alternated from one side of the hall to the other. Lester's room was the second door on the right. Essie pulled out the master key from her trousers and slipped it into the lock. It opened easily. She carefully pushed open the door and she and Marjorie entered the injured man's room.

"Shut the door," ordered Essie as she rolled her walker into the center of the apartment. "It's pretty much the same arrangement as mine."

"Mine too," said Marjorie. "All the rooms have the same pattern. Only the furniture and decorations are different. What are we looking for?"

"I don't know, Marjorie," replied Essie annoyed. "If I knew, then I'd go right to it. Just look around and see if you see anything strange or anything that will tell us something about Mr. Mills or who might want to hurt him."

The two women began to investigate. Essie rolled into the bedroom and Marjorie centered her sleuthing on the living room and kitchenette. The apartment was clean, neat, and organized. There were not many decorations, but then Mr. Mills had not been at Happy Haven long and hadn't had a lot of time to accumulate many mementos.

In the bedroom, Essie discovered a simple layout. There was a single bed and one nightstand with a lamp. On the nightstand, Essie couldn't help but notice a crossword puzzle book just like hers. *So, a kindred spirit,* she thought. On the far wall there was a long low dresser. There was also a host of framed photographs on the wall above the dresser. There wasn't much order to them. It was as if Lester had arrived with a lot of family pictures and had just hung them all on the wall, helter skelter. Essie began at one end and examined the photographs, one by one, trying to get a sense of the man, and what he was like. She discovered an abundance of photos of a beautiful woman, some of the woman at a much younger age and then others following her as she became older. There were individual pictures of this woman and many photos of the woman with a man who was obviously Lester. Essie found what was no doubt their wedding picture, even though the bride was not wearing traditional wedding garb. The couple were simply dressed, and the woman was carrying a small bouquet. It was true that Lester was noticeably older than his wife in their wedding photo. Lester looked about fifty and the woman looked barely thirty. Essie was struck by the number of pictures that Lester Mills maintained of his deceased wife. There were only a few photographs of their children. She found mostly baby photographs and pictures of their children from school. On the wall above the far right edge of the dresser were what appeared to be family photographs with Lester's wife and children; some were taken outdoors, some in restaurants and some in a living room. There was one that did not include the wife. In this photograph, the children were adults and Lester appeared much older and much more somber than he did in the other pictures.

Essie studied this photograph. This was the only picture that she'd found so far in which she realized that she actually recognized Lester's children—the ones she'd seen with him at the elevator the other day and later—in the elevator. *It must be a fairly recent picture,* she thought.

"Essie!" called Marjorie, from the living room, "are you finding anything?"

"No!" yelled back Essie. "How about you?"

"Nothing! Lester Mills is very neat and not much of a saver."

"Except for photographs," said Essie to herself. She examined the picture. It was a large portrait. In it, Lester was sitting in an arm chair and the three children were standing around him. None of the four were smiling. Lester, in fact, looked quite morose. Essie got the impression that he felt as though he was in jail and the children were his jailers. She stared at each of the children. They looked like well bred, proper, mature children. The boys were wearing suits. *They're clean shaven without any of those disgusting beards or tattoos or ear rings,* thought Essie. She liked men like that. The girl was also neat and looked well mannered with her hands folded primly in from of her. Essie noticed she was wearing a gold ring with a ruby on her right hand, so she assumed the daughter was single. Focusing in on the ruby ring, Essie pulled her eyes close to the daughter's ears where she discovered that Ms. Mills was also wearing a pair of golden ruby earrings. A pair of earrings that Essie recognized.

"Marjorie!" she called. "Come! Look at this!" When Marjorie came into the bedroom, Essie pointed out the photograph to her and waited while Marjorie stared at the family portrait.

"What, Essie?" asked Marjorie, after looking at the picture for a while. "So, this is Lester and his children, I'm guessing."

"Don't you see anything?" Essie asked.

"Three nicely-dressed young people and a handsome older gentleman," said Marjorie, with a wicked glint in her eyes.

"No, Marjorie," said Essie. "Look closer. Something else. Something you've seen."

"What?" said Marjorie, "You're the detective, Essie. Just tell me."

"Look at the girl's ears," demanded Essie, poking at the photograph up on the wall with her finger.

"Oh!" cried Marjorie. "She has on that earring you found."

"Bravo, Marjorie," said Essie. "Now you're a detective."

A loud knock on the door sounded, and the two women quickly exited Lester's bedroom and then his apartment and walked calmly but quickly back to the hallway intersection where Opal and Fay were waiting.

"Why did you knock?" whispered Essie to Opal, but Opal just made a "come here" gesture to them and led them around the corner towards the elevator. There, they could all see Phyllis on her hands and knees in front of the elevator.

"Phyllis!" cried Essie coming up to the desk clerk. "Did you lose something?"

"I think I dropped my master key up here when I was up here checking on Mr. Mills' room earlier. I remember thinking I dropped something when I was getting back into the elevator. Oh, I don't remember. It could have happened anywhere. I'll be in terrible trouble if I don't find it."

"Oh, no!" cried Essie. "Here, let us help you look for it. Come on, ladies, let's help Phyllis *find* that master key." Essie used her walker to bend down on the ground with Phyllis, and the other two did also, but begrudgingly. Fay sat in her wheelchair, looking mystified.

"Where could it be?" asked Phyllis, the sound of terror in her voice, as she patted the thick carpet by the elevator with her fingers.

"Oh, I'm *sure* we'll find it," assured Essie, also patting around and nodding so that the others did the same. After a few moments of fake searching, Essie reached under a bench near the wall by the elevator and cried, "Oh, is this it, Phyllis?" She held up the gold master key with the tag that she'd had in her trouser pocket all along.

"Oh my, Essie! You've saved my life. Thank you so much." Phyllis helped Essie up from the floor and gave her a little hug.

"Oh, it's nothing," remarked Essie, looking around at the sneering faces of her friends.

Chapter 19

Later, back in Essie's room, the four friends all plopped down on Essie's comfortable furniture. Essie stretched out in her recliner, her walker at the ready. Fay sat in her wheelchair between the chairs.

"Essie!" cried Marjorie, "I can't believe you extricated yourself from that little mess so easily."

"Yes," agreed Opal. "If Phyllis had discovered that you were the one who'd stolen her master key, she'd be furious. Who knows what she'd do?"

"Luckily," said Essie with a deep sigh, "we won't have to find out."

"You won't be able to snatch her master key again," said Marjorie, shaking her head. "I'm afraid that's the last we'll be able to search Lester's room."

"I should hope so," cried Opal. "It's terrible that we did it once."

"Oh, calm down, Opal," said Essie. "You weren't involved. If anyone would have gotten in trouble, it would have been Marjorie and me. You and Fay were just look-outs. You were never in danger."

"I *felt* like I was in danger," replied Opal. "I hope all of that was worth it, Essie."

"I believe it was. Right, Marjorie?"

"Go on, Essie, show her," said Marjorie, waving her hand at Essie.

"What?" asked Opal. "Did you two find something?"

"Essie did," said Marjorie.

Essie edged forward in her recliner and reached into her pocket and brought out the gold ruby earring.

"I wish you wouldn't carry that thing around, Essie," said Opal when she saw the earring. "It's obviously very valuable and the owner must be looking for it all over."

"Yes, she must," agreed Essie, "and we now believe we know who that owner is."

"Who?" asked Opal.

"Lester Mills' daughter. We saw a photograph of her hanging on the wall in Lester's bedroom and she was wearing this exact same earring."

"Are you sure, Essie?" asked Opal, cautiously. She frowned and continued to stare at the earring. "But, that means that . . ."

"It means that Lester's daughter was out in that field and lost her earring there," said Essie.

"And that she was probably involved in shooting off that rocket that hit Lester," added Marjorie.

"We have to tell the detectives," said Opal. She rose and walked over to Essie's landline telephone.

"Wait!" cried Essie, placing her hand on Opal's. "Let's think about this a minute."

"What's there to think about, Essie?" demanded Opal. "We have an important clue in this mystery. We have an obligation to inform the police."

"If we tell them we found that earring in the field, we'll be admitting that we were exploring around in a crime scene," argued Essie.

"No, we weren't," replied Marjorie, "There wasn't any police tape there. There was no sign or anything indicating that we couldn't go into that field, Essie. Yes, maybe we shouldn't have, but we weren't committing a crime. I agree with Opal. We need to report this—all of this—to the detectives."

"And by *all* of this, you mean, *everything* we found in the field as well as what we just discovered in Lester's room?" asked Essie. "The piece of paper with the formulas, the earring, and the fact that a photograph of Lester's children in his bedroom shows his daughter wearing this same earring?"

"Yes!" replied both Opal and Marjorie.

"I'm not so sure it's a good idea," said Essie, "but I'm certainly, if nothing else, a team player."

"Ha!" cried Opal. "You go off on your own little tangents more than anyone else I know, Essie. You stole Phyllis's master key before you even mentioned to us about searching Lester's room. You really didn't give us a chance to even discuss your plan. You just forced us into it."

"Sloopy doopy, Opal," said Essie, "If I waited for all of you to get on board, nothing would ever get done around here."

"Do you have anything to eat, Essie?" asked Marjorie, changing the topic. "All that sleuthing has made me hungry."

"See that secretary desk beside you," replied Essie, shrugging her shoulders at her scatterbrained buddy. "Open the top drawer. There's some chocolates in there I just got as a prize for a crossword puzzle contest I won a while back."

"You won a contest?" asked Opal. "You mean one at Happy Haven?"

"No," said Essie. "It was something I found online and I entered it and I won those candies. I don't really care that much for candy, so I put it in there in case my grandchildren came over and wanted some, but Marjorie, you're something like my grandchildren, so you might as well eat them." Essie gave Marjorie a superior smile as Marjorie flung open the drawer and removed a small box covered in what looked like green velvet.

"Since when do you enter online contests, Essie?" asked Marjorie, examining the box. She removed the lid and gasped. "Ooo, these look yummy!"

"My grandson Ned showed me how," replied Essie. "I'd really just rather win more puzzle books, but if people want to send me free stuff, I'll take it. Go at it, Marjorie. Eat it all if you want."

Marjorie selected one of the chocolates and took a dainty bite.

"Yum!" she cried. "This is fabulous! It's much better than the kind you normally get at Valentine's Day from your family."

"Oh, give me one of those," demanded Opal, rising from her arm chair and heading over to Marjorie. Marjorie held out the little box to Opal, who examined the various chocolates and then selected a dark one in the shape of a crescent. She took a bite and sat back down in her arm chair. "This is good. Hmm. Now, Essie, back to business. We've procrastinated enough over your candies. Are you going to call those detectives or shall I?"

"I'll do it," said Essie, resigned. She got up, rolled over to her desk and sat down. She opened her telephone book and located the number for the local police department. She dialed the number and a receptionist answered.

"Reardon Police Department, Sargent Gomez speaking."

"I'd like to speak to Detective Blake . . . or Detective Farley," said Essie. The receptionist quickly connected her to the detectives. Farley answered.

"Oh, Detective Farley?" asked Essie. "This is Essie Cobb, from the Happy Haven Retirement Center. You interviewed me and some of my friends about that firecracker that landed on Mr. Mills on the Fourth of July this afternoon . . ."

"Tell them to come over, Essie," said Opal, breaking in. "We shouldn't do this over the phone."

"Yes, Detective," replied Essie, trying to listen to the voice on the phone, holding up her hand to Opal. "Yes, actually, we do have some new information for you. You will? Oh, that would be fine. Yes, all four of us are here in my room—3B. It's just off the lobby to the right."

After her phone call, Essie told the women that the two detectives would be right over.

"Well, that's service," said Marjorie. "How often do you have civil servants respond that quickly? And at night?" Now on her second chocolate, she rubbed some of the drippy cherry filling from the corner of her mouth.

"They *are* trying to solve what may turn out to be attempted murder," said Opal.

"Ooo, it's so gruesome," said Marjorie, cringing. "I think I need another one of these chocolates."

"Don't hog them all, Marjorie," said Opal, "Give me another. You've had two already." Marjorie bent over, stretching her body out to hand the box to Opal, and Opal reached her hand out as far as it would go but she couldn't reach the box. The two women laughed at their predicament.

"What's wrong with you two?" demanded Essie. "You're being ridiculous."

"You're the ridiculous one," said Opal, getting up finally and plodding over to Marjorie for another chocolate. She grabbed one and turned to go, then had another thought and reached back and grabbed a second one. Taking a big bite out of one, she looked at its interior, and said, "Ooo! This one's mint. I love mint!"

She nestled down into the arm chair and lifted one leg over the arm rest.

"Opal!" cried Essie, looking at her proper friend's behavior. "What is wrong with you?"

Nothing," replied Opal. "I'm just relaxing. Yum! That was delish. Ooo! Marjorie! Look at this one. It's caramel." She took a nibble from her third chocolate and a very runny caramel crème oozed out of the center. Laughing, Opal slurped up the liquid as some of it dribbled onto her cashmere sweater.

"He he," laughed Marjorie, "Opal is a slob. Opal is a slob." She pointed at the mess Opal was making as she herself gobbled up her third chocolate without spilling any of its interior. Opal and Marjorie were now laughing and giggling hysterically.

"What is wrong with you two?" demanded Essie. "The detectives will be here any minute. Fay, are you seeing this?" Essie looked at Fay, who was glancing back and forth between Marjorie and Opal, her eyes wide open.

"Oh, rooty tooty!" cried Essie, slapping her hand on her forehead. "I bet I know." She pulled herself out of her rocker and rolled her walker over to Marjorie. Grabbing the box of chocolates from her friend's hands, she stormed back to her own chair with the confiscated goods.

"Essie!" cried Marjorie, "You said we could eat them."

"That was before I realized what they contained," said Essie, turning the box over and reading the bottom. "Just as I thought. Every one of these little devils contains alcohol. Or as it's phrased on the cover, *liqueur.* You're both *drunk!* Opal evidently more so than you, Marjorie." She took the box of chocolates and tossed it in a waste basket next to her rocker. "Now what do we do? The detectives will be here any minute."

"We'll be fine, Essie," said Marjorie, stretching out in her chair, "I can hold my liquor. I only had a few sips or bites—or whatever." She giggled. "I can't speak for Opal. She's a teetotaler."

"I am fine, oh, so fine," intoned Opal, slurring her words, now with both legs draped over the edge of Essie's large gold arm chair. Essie could see the edge of Opal's panties, not something she thought anyone should view.

"You are not fine, Opal," replied Essie, rising. "Come on, both of you. Up!"

"Why?" whined Opal, "I'm so comfy here. You have the best chairs, Essie. I could sleep on your chairs." She stretched her body out width-wise so her head was draped over one arm of the chair.

"Get up, Opal!" yelled Essie to her friend, "You're going to walk this off now!" Essie pulled, unsuccessfully, on Opal's legs in an attempt to place them on the ground in a more lady-like pose. "Stand up, Opal!"

"I'll help you, Essie!" shouted Marjorie, jumping up. "Come on, Opal! Let's march!" Marjorie started marching around Essie's small living room in time to an unheard beat. Fay sat befuddled in her wheelchair near the kitchen just staring at her friends and their strange antics.

"Opal, get up this instant!" demanded Essie. She gave one last pull which dethroned Opal from her seat, launching the two women backwards and both onto the floor.

At that moment, there was a knock at the door, and it opened slightly. Detective Farley stuck her head inside.

"Anyone home?" she called. "We heard a lot of noise. Is everyone okay?"

Chapter 20

"Oh, my! Miss Essie! Miss Opal!" cried out Detective Farley as she and her partner Blake entered quickly into Essie's living room. The two detectives quickly rushed over to the two women on the floor and helped them to their feet. "What happened?"

"Are you ladies all right?" asked Blake, helping Opal and Essie into chairs.

"We're fine," huffed Essie. "Some people just can't hold their *chocolate*."

"I'm afraid I don't understand. . ." said Farley, glancing in an amused fashion to Blake.

"Never mind, detectives," declared Marjorie, standing by the window and out of the fray. "We're glad you got here so fast." She gestured for them to be seated and the two police officers positioned themselves on Essie's sofa.

"You said you had new information for us?" asked Blake. He pulled out his trusty notebook.

"Oh!" cried Opal. "I got chocolate all over my chin, Essie." She rubbed her chin and looked at the residue of the chocolate truffle remaining on her finger. Then she licked her finger. "Yum."

"Good grief, Opal," declared Marjorie. "Pull it together, woman."

"Um, yes, Detective," replied Essie to the detective's question, in an attempt to divert his attention away from Opal's lack of manners. "We actually have found some clues that we believe you should see . . ."

"Oh?" said Blake. Both detectives scooted forward on the couch and looked at Essie intently.

"I'm not sure how to say this . . ." began Essie, " but after I returned from the hospital this morning, we all decided that we should go over to that field up the street and see if we could find any evidence of those hoodlums who shot at us with that firecracker . . ."

"Yes, hoodlums!" shouted Opal, waving the handkerchief from the cuff of her sweater like a victory flag.

"Marjorie, can't you take her somewhere?" asked Essie, *sotto voce*. "She's embarrassing herself."

"I think she's funny," replied Marjorie. "Opal, take a nap," Marjorie ordered Opal, who glared at her in return and then hunkered down in her chair like a scolded child. The detectives glanced at each other with knowing looks.

"Anyway," continued Essie, "we all walked down the street to the field, and Marjorie and I found a pathway into the field. Opal and Fay remained on the sidewalk in case we got lost or needed help."

"That was a wise idea," added Farley.

"It was a foolish idea," said Blake to his partner, disagreeing. The moonlight pouring in from Essie's picture window reflected off his bald brown pate.

"Be that as it may," Essie soldiered on, "we did search the field. We followed what looked to us like a fairly well-worn path that entered from the sidewalk and followed it around. We ended up in a small clearing where we found a lot of trash, but nothing we considered a meaningful clue."

"So," added Marjorie, obviously wanting to put in her two cents, "we took a different fork in the pathway and eventually came to another little clearing."

"Yes," agreed Essie. "That one was much smaller and hadn't seen so many visitors. Marjorie and I both searched around, and we believe this was the location where the person shot off the rocket that hit Mr. Mills.

While we were there we found a few items that we believe might be clues to the identity of the person who set off the rocket."

"And do you have these clues now?" asked Blake, pointedly.

"Yes," said Essie, rising. She shoved her walker over to him and reached into her pocket. She pulled out the folded up piece of paper. "This small piece of paper. It looks like it might be some teenager's homework assignment because there are lots of math symbols and formulas. We thought it was maybe geometry then, but now we're not so sure after I did some computer research."

"Definitely geometry," observed Marjorie, "and much too complicated for me." She giggled and smiled at the male detective Blake, who took the paper and grimaced at the complex symbols on the paper.

"That's not all," Essie continued. "We also found this earring." She reached into her pocket and brought out the gold and ruby earring. "We found it quite close to where we found the math paper."

"Miss Essie," began Farley, "your efforts are appreciated, but our forensics unit went all over that field. They obviously didn't find these items."

"Then your forensics unit is incompetent," mumbled Opal in her huddled up position in her arm chair.

"What?" asked Blake.

"What Opal means, Detective," said Essie, with an embarrassed laugh, "is that if two old ladies can track down these clues in fifteen minutes. . . ."

"We should hire *you* to do our evidence gathering?" asked Blake. He puffed out his chest, which stretched his uniform shirt almost past its capability to hold in his muscles.

"Yes," gushed Marjorie.

"Actually," Essie began, "we'd just like you to consider this earring, which we believe is a direct link to Mr. Mills' daughter."

"And how would you know that?" asked Farley.

"Hmmm," said Essie hesitating. "Well, you see, once we found this paper and this earring, we were determined to find out more about these clues. So, earlier this evening, we popped into Mr. Mills' apartment and sort of peeked around . . ."

"Into his apartment?" asked Blake. "Did he invite you in? That would be hard to do as he's presently in a coma in the hospital."

"We know that, Detective," replied Marjorie. "But, you see, here at Happy Haven, we're all just one big happy family. That's why we call it *Happy* Haven. My apartment is your apartment. Your apartment is my apartment. I mean, right now, we're all here in Essie's room, but we could just as well be in my room or Opal's or Fay's. I'm sure Mr. Mills wouldn't mind if we were in his apartment."

"Did you ask him?" asked Blake.

"Well, no. . ." said Marjorie.

"That's not the point," interjected Essie. "We couldn't ask him because he's unconscious and unable to answer any questions, but he knows Opal really, really well. They're good friends and were good friends before they came here to Happy Haven. We're sure he wouldn't mind if she went into his apartment. And besides, the reason we went into his place was to help find out who had hurt him. I'm sure he wouldn't mind if we did that."

"Ed," whispered Farley to her partner, "they've already broken and entered. Let's find out what they discovered and then when we see what they have—if anything—we can determine what to do with them."

"All right," snorted Blake, contorting his mouth around as he contemplated the legalities and ethical conundrums involved in the ladies' behavior.

"As I was saying," continued Essie, "we went into Mr. Mills' room. There's a framed photograph of Mr. Mills with his children hanging on the wall in his bedroom. In the photograph," said Essie, "I could clearly see his daughter wearing what appears to be a pair of earrings that perfectly match this one that we discovered out in the field. Now, doesn't that mean that she must have been there? We believe that Mr. Mills' children—or at least one of them—were the ones who shot off that rocket."

"Miss Essie," said Farley, standing, "we'll have to take those clues." She reached out her hand and Essie placed the math paper and the earring in her palm. The detective pulled a clear plastic bag from her vest pocket, deposited the items inside and placed the bag back into her jacket.

"So?" asked Essie. "Will these clues solve the case? Will you be able to arrest Mills' children for attempted murder?"

"It's not so easy," replied Blake, stretching his torso and placing a hand on his hip. "At the moment, it's just circumstantial evidence. There could be any number of reasons why that earring was in that field. Even if we can prove that this particular earring actually belongs to Mills' daughter, we don't know when she dropped it in the field, or even *if* she was the one who dropped it there. It could have happened days or weeks ago."

"We've found no motive for the children to hurt their father," added Farley. "I don't suppose you ladies came across a *motive* in your sleuthing, did you?" She glanced anxiously from one face to another but none of the four senior citizens provided her with any positive response.

"If you *had* a motive," suggested Essie, "then our clues—the paper and the earring—would mean something?"

"It would certainly all tie in together better," agreed Farley, obviously wanting the little group of amateur detectives to feel as if their endeavors had not been in vain.

"Lord, don't encourage them, Beth," said Blake, wincing. He scratched his thick mustache.

Farley just smiled at her partner and at the four elderly ladies.

"Well, that's good to know," said Essie, nodding her head. "Now, would you detectives like some tea? I can brew some water up in my kitchenette. I have a supply of several different types of tea." She rolled her walker over to her kitchen cupboard and brought down a teak box. Setting it on the counter and opening it, multi-colored bags of tea were revealed. Essie turned to the stove and flipped on the heat under the burner below her teapot.

"Oh, thank you, Miss Essie," said Farley, coming over to the kitchen, "but we really must be getting on our way."

"Yes," agreed Blake, joining her, "and no more sleuthing out in fields for you ladies—*or* breaking into other residents' apartments!" He pointed his finger at each of them.

"Truly, Essie, and *all* of you," said Farley sincerely, "it's quite possible that we may be dealing with attempted murder here. If that's so, you all need to be careful. Don't do anything foolish."

"*And* to calm your concerns about Mr. Mills," added Blake, "we've placed a guard outside his hospital room."

"So you *do* think he's in danger?" asked Essie. "You *do* think we're dealing with attempted murder and not just an accident?"

"We're not ruling anything out," replied Blake.

"Is he still in a coma?" asked Marjorie.

"He was when we last checked an hour or so ago," added Farley.

"Poor Lester!" cried Opal, burying her head in her hands and sobbing profusely.

With a final glance at Opal, the two detectives headed out of Essie's apartment, closing the door quietly behind them.

"Oh no!" cried Opal as soon as the detectives were gone, bolting upright, and pulling her knees up to her chest. "We're in trouble! Essie, what are we going to do?"

"Revel devil!" cried Essie. "How drunk can one person get on a few pieces of liquor-infused candy?"

"Obviously, Opal has little experience with alcohol," said Marjorie with a shrug. "She's not as worldly as I am."

"You're fine, Opal," said Essie loudly to Opal and she pulled Opal's legs down so her pose was more discreet. "I'm making you some tea, so just sit there and be quiet. We'll try to sober you up. Marjorie, help me out here."

Essie set out tea cups and saucers and poured hot water in each. Marjorie came over to the kitchen and carried the tray to the coffee table and Essie brought the teak box of tea bags along in the basket of her walker.

All four ladies were delighted as they each selected a tea bag from the wooden box and placed it in their cup of hot water. Marjorie chose passion fruit. Opal chose licorice. Fay chose mint. Essie chose apricot. Then the four of them settled back and sipped their beverages and planned their next move.

Chapter 21

After breakfast the next morning, Essie made another secretive phone call to her grandson, but this time about a new problem. Shortly after she'd finished her morning crossword puzzle, Ned arrived, knocking on her door and immediately poked his head inside.

"Oh, Ned!" said Essie, "Come in. I just finished my puzzle." She held up her crossword book to show her grandson her accomplishment.

"That's great, Grandma!" said Ned, quietly shutting her front door behind him. He was carrying a paper bag with handles. The logo of a wireless phone company was emblazoned on the side.

"What's that?" she asked.

"The answer to your request," replied Ned, coming over to her and setting the bag on her coffee table.

"I thought I asked you to help me find out more information on Lester Mills and his company—and his children," Essie added, her face a mass of questions. "What is it?"

"Grandma," began Ned, "we've been going round and round about this, and I just decided that instead of trying to *convince* you to get a smart phone, I'd just get you one myself. As a matter of fact, I just added you to my monthly plan for virtually nothing . . ."

"Oh, Ned!" cried Essie, "you can't afford to do that."

"But I *can*, Grandma," answered Ned, placing his hands on hers which were fluttering around with her concern. "And besides, you *need* a smart phone. I mean, Essie Cobb, senior sleuth! How can you do any real proper detecting without a good phone? Any gumshoe worth her salt knows that." He bent his head down and gave her a pointed look.

"I just thought *you* could help me search on the Happy Haven computer," said Essie sheepishly. "Maybe I'm not looking in the right place or the right way."

"Maybe not, Grandma," said Ned nodding, "but any searching we can do on those old clunkers in the HH computer room, we can do and then some on *this* little number." He reached into the sack and brought out a shiny box with fancy lettering and a photo of a smart phone on the front. Quickly, he unwrapped the package and revealed to Essie a sleek black and silver rectangle with a TV-like face. "Grandma! Meet your new best friend. Your smartphone." Pressing a few buttons, Ned quickly brought Essie's new cellphone to life. "Now, let me introduce you to what this baby can do."

"You make it sound like it's a miracle worker," said Essie cautiously.

"It is, Grandma," gushed Ned. "Now first, of course, it's a phone. Let's start at the beginning. Here's how you make a phone call." He showed her the buttons to press to type in a phone number and the button to send the number. He showed her what would happen when she received a call."

"It will ring when someone calls you," Ned said. "Here's your new number. I think the logical thing is to get rid of your landline—and your answering machine."

"My answering machine!" cried Essie. "I just figured out how to use it. Your Mom and your aunt will have a fit if I get rid of my answering machine. They want me to be available whenever they call, and if I'm not here, they want to be able to leave a message. It's downright like a penitentiary some times, if you ask me."

"I totally understand, Grandma," agreed Ned, "but this smartphone will *solve* that problem for you. You just keep it with you at all times and you'll never have to miss a call again and, therefore, never really need an answering machine."

"But, Ned," cried Essie, pouting, "I liked the answering machine. It kept your mother off my back. I mean, it made your mother feel more comfortable about my whereabouts and she wasn't always bothering me. Now, I'll have to talk to her whenever she calls, and, Ned, she calls a *lot*."

"No, you won't, Grandma," replied Ned, holding the new phone out in front of Essie. "See this button here. You press this if you get a call from Mom and you don't want to talk to her. It will send her call to voice mail and she can leave you a message if she wants. She won't know why you can't answer your phone. Then you can play it back later, *if* you want. But the good thing is, with the smartphone, you can *see* who's calling you. So, if you don't want to talk to the person or if it's a salesperson—or Mom—just don't answer. If it's your boyfriend, you can answer it right away."

"Oh, Ned, don't be silly. So, how do I do that?" she asked.

"This button," he said, showing her how to tell who was calling, how to send a call to voice-mail and how to respond if she wanted.

"Bird's word!" declared Essie. "This phone can do everything but my dishes, it seems."

"Oh, we're just getting started," said Ned. "Are you ready to see its search capabilities?" Essie nodded excitedly. "Okay, let's check out that Lester Mills you seem so interested in." Ned brought up a search engine page and started typing in terms. Quickly, he flipped through pages of information on Lester Mills and Mills Electronics, his firm.

"What does it say?" she asked. "I found a lot of this information already—and Opal tracked down quite a bit of material on Lester's background."

"Well, it seems that his firm is fairly large. It's not Reardon's largest employer, but still, it's doing quite well. Says Mills started it back in 1970. He's been the CEO from the beginning, until recently when his oldest son took on the post of COO—that's Chief Operating Officer, Grandma. Doesn't say about the other two children you mentioned. Oh, down here, look. The wife died here. Not much about her, but it does seem the children have been involved in running the company in recent years."

"I don't know if that helps us determine who targeted Lester with that rocket—or why. It might be anyone. It might be someone at his company, or it could be someone else for a reason totally unrelated to his business," suggested Essie.

"True," agreed Ned. He pushed some more buttons, adding more search terms.

"What are you doing?" Essie asked, watching his fingers fly over the small device.

"I'm not giving up on the business angle just yet," said Ned. "Let's take a look at just how successful Mills Electronics is—or claims to be." He jumped to another site. "This is a Wall Street site that provides analyses of various companies for investors who might be considering putting money into that business. It ranks and rates each business. Here. Look! Mills Electronics gets a 92. That's really good. And it's gone up recently. Wonder why?"

"You mean more people are investing in Lester's company?" asked Essie.

"Yes," replied Ned, "which suggests that they're doing something right or are making a major move or something important is about to happen to the company. It could be a takeover or just a major expansion. Hmm. Let me check something else." Ned pressed more buttons and brought up more sites. One was full of lots of numbers and formulas. Ned became engrossed. "Oh, sorry, Grandma. This probably looks like gibberish to you," he said, "but to a computer science geek like me, it's just everyday stuff."

"Actually, Ned," said Essie, squinting at the page of numbers, "it looks a little familiar."

"How so?" he asked her, turning to look at her face.

"Did I mention the clues that I found out in the field?"

"What?"

"Oh, it's nothing much," she replied when she saw Ned's face become suddenly worried when she mentioned the word *field*, "but I found this piece of paper out there where I thought maybe they shot that rocket. At first, we thought it was some teenager's math homework, but then we realized that it was more— more like this," she declared, pointing her finger at the screen on the phone.

"Really?" asked Ned. "Do you recognize any part of it?"

"I remember seeing that little swirly gig," said Essie, pointing to a symbol, "and also that one." She pointed again at the screen.

"Hmm," said Ned. "Do you have that little piece of paper?"

"Nope, sorry," replied Essie. "I gave it to the detectives who were investigating the rocket hitting Mr. Mills. That and the earring."

"The earring?"

"We also found an earring in the field."

"Grandma!" cried Ned. "You really have been investigating."

"Of course," said Essie. "That's what I do."

"If what was on that paper you found is anything at all related to what's on this page on this site, then I think you need to know what this article is discussing."

"What?" she asked.

"This is an article discussing new developments in drone technology," he replied. "Do you know what that is?"

"I've learned quite a bit about it lately."

Ned continued, "Right now drones are mostly being used by the military for surveillance and targeting, but there are private companies that are presently investigating the possibility of using drones for civilian purposes. I think that little piece of paper you found may have been describing the set up and manipulation of a small drone . . ."

"You mean a drone that could shoot a rocket into the bottom of a man on the front yard of the Happy Haven Retirement Center?" asked Essie.

"Exactly," replied Ned. He quickly pushed more buttons. A screen popped up with the words, "Mills Electronics" at the top. Ned rolled the page down. On the left, were photographs of various strange devices with descriptions of their capabilities and uses on the right. As Ned scrolled down, some of the photos of the devices were blacked out along with their descriptions and over the black squares was written the word *classified.* "It seems to me, Grandma, that we may have discovered the firecracker that attacked Lester Mills— or one quite like it. And it's a firecracker, or I should say *rocket*, that *his* company probably developed. That is, developed for the military."

"Oh, and Ned," cried Essie, "when the detectives questioned us all about the rocket and what we saw—of course, I didn't see anything—but Opal saw it coming down and she tried to describe it, and Fay saw it but she couldn't describe it. But she made a drawing of the rocket for the detectives, and I remember that Fay's drawing had the letters *ME* and some numbers on it. I didn't know what it meant at the time, but now, it seems to me that *ME* must stand for *Mills Electronics*."

"It certainly does," agreed Ned. "You can see the letters on this particular drone model here." He pointed to one of the small images.

"But why would Lester build one of these drones and then have it shoot him in the rear?" asked Essie as if it were the most obvious question, because, of course, it was.

"That's the 100 thousand dollar question, Grandma," said Ned with a sigh. "Obviously, something is going on over at Mills Electronics—and you and I are going to find out what that something is."

"We are? How?" she asked

"We're going to go undercover," replied her grandson.

Chapter 22

Later that day, Essie hurried back to her room from lunch. She wanted to be somewhere private when Ned called on her new smart phone. Earlier, the twosome had worked out a plan whereby Ned would apply for a job at Mills Electronics. Ned said he'd read that the company was hiring people for its computer division and that was Ned's specialty. Of course, Ned already had a job he loved and had no intention of actually working for Mills Electronics, even if he could get employed there. He only wanted to check out the facility and then report back to Essie what he found out.

Ned had taken the day off from his regular job so he could conduct this sleuthing adventure for his grandmother. Essie felt somewhat guilty, but not too guilty, for making her grandson fib to his boss like this. She really liked that she and Ned seemed to be kindred spirits and shared a love of adventure. Of course, her daughter Claudia, Ned's mother, didn't share this same love, so Essie knew she'd have to protect Ned from his mother ever finding out about how he was assisting her.

Essie had barely plopped herself down in her comfy recliner and pulled up the footrest when her new smart phone rang from inside the pocket of her trousers. She quickly reached for it and looked at the screen. It informed her that *Ned* was calling her. As Ned had showed her, she pressed the answer button and put the device to her ear.

"Hello, Ned," she said, "is that you?"

"Hi, Grandma!" replied Ned's voice. "I have to whisper. I'm alone here in a conference room at Mills Electronics."

"They left you alone?" Essie asked.

"Yes, they had me take some aptitude tests and now I'm just waiting to be interviewed."

"Have you found out anything about Lester or his children?" she asked impatiently.

"Hang on, Grandma," he whispered. "One thing at a time. It's great that I've gotten in here at the company. I'm going to try to snoop around a little. Maybe speak to an employee if I can find one."

"Okay, but don't do anything to put yourself in danger," reminded Essie.

"Don't worry," said Ned quickly. "Gotta go. Someone's coming!"

With that, the little sign on her phone indicating Ned's call vanished. Essie sat there staring at her phone. As Ned had showed her the other day, she brought up the search engine box and entered some terms. She typed in *Lester Mills* and *Mills Electronics*. Soon the little screen on her smart phone was filled with articles about the company and its founder. She methodically began with the first article and began to read. It appeared to be what she'd once heard someone call a *fluff piece,* lauding the outstanding contributions of the company to the country's success. Mills Electronics had produced numerous devices and mechanisms that were presently being used in science and industry to produce goods and improve various products. She tapped on each article in turn and one after the other seemed to present the same material in different words. By the time she'd reached the fifth article, she felt she'd almost memorized the many wonderful accomplishments of Mills Electronics. Nothing she discovered seemed to confirm the discussion she'd overheard between Lester and his children at the elevator about the company being in trouble.

At the bottom of the page was an article entitled, "Mills Electronics Not Interested in Military Contract?" Essie tapped on that piece, as it seemed different from the previous five she'd just read. She quickly perused the paragraphs. Apparently, it appeared that the U. S. Military was interested in having Mills Electronics do some work for them, but Mills had declined their request. The article was short and no reason was given for Mills' lack of interest in the government work. Essie wondered why a successful company wouldn't want a government contract if they were offered one. She glanced up and down the page of sources and then pressed the arrow that led to the second page of articles. Here she also ran her eyes down the list of articles, trying to find any other source that might provide more information about the potential government contract that Mills had rejected.

At that moment, her phone rang again and the bubble with Ned's name in it popped up on the phone's screen. Essie pressed the answer button and Ned's voice came on.

"Grandma!" he said in an excited whisper, "I just finished my interview with one of the managers here and it looks like they want to hire me. They really liked my resume. Can you believe it? I mean, I'm just doing this to—you know—and I get a job offer. Without even a second interview."

"Oh my, Ned! That's wonderful, I guess, or should I say, that's terrible," moaned Essie. "I don't know what to say."

"Yeah," he replied. "They asked me to wait back in this conference room again because they want me to speak to one of their executives. That would be one of the children, wouldn't it?"

"It must be!" cried Essie. "Oh, Ned, that would be amazing if you could talk to one of Lester's children and maybe find out what they're up to, if you could—*if* they're up to anything . . ."

"I did manage to speak with the secretary who brought me in to see the HR manager. She was very friendly, and I tried to grill her without seeming to be grilling her, if you know what I mean," he reported. "I said I was surprised that they were so anxious to hire me and that it all seemed to be moving so fast and she said something about there being a *shake-up* and new management wanting to move in a different direction."

"Do you think she meant new management such as Lester's children?" asked Essie.

"Well, I hope to find out on this second interview," said Ned. "Wish me luck."

"I do, Ned," replied Essie, "and, Ned, be careful! Remember, we suspect his children—or at least one of them—of causing their father's accident. They could be dangerous."

"Don't worry, Grandma. I'll be careful."

Ned clicked off and Essie returned to her list of articles about Mills Electronics. She kept hitting the forward arrow button to see how many more articles there were. There appeared to be about four pages worth. Essie checked the titles of all four pages of articles but no other article bore a headline that connected Mills to a military contract. *Hmm*, she thought to herself, *I wonder*. She went back to the search engine box and erased the search terms *Lester Mills* and *Mills Electronics*. This time she wrote in *Mills Electronics* and *government*. When she pressed the button, the screen filled with several articles. She could see immediately that most were identical if not similar. However, the top article was dated just *hours* ago and was not from a newspaper, but from an online site. Essie wondered if such a source was reputable as its name was *Daily Doings in Washington. Hmm*, she thought, *sounds like a gossip column.*

She clicked on the source and read, "Word from the Pentagon is that small engineering firm Mills Electronics has just been signed to a contract with the military to produce the government's new mini-drone rocket, to be used in remote targeting of enemy combatants. . ." Essie gasped, but continued reading. The rest of the short article was mostly conjecture about the terms of the deal and how much Mills would likely make from the new contract. Speculation was that the company would profit a lot. There was nothing in the short gossipy report about *who* at Mills had forged and signed the contract—if indeed such a contract existed.

Essie read and re-read the little article. She then continued her online search to see if she could find out any more information about this so-called *mini-drone rocket* and Mills Electronics' new contract to produce it. She wished she could question Lester Mills about it.

Just then, her smart phone rang again. Essie saw Ned's name and quickly answered it.

"Hi, Grams!" he said in a much more jaunty voice than before.

"You sound good, Ned," said Essie. "Did you have your interview with one of the Mills' children?"

"Did I," he replied. "I'm on my way back home now. In fact, I'm almost to your place. I'm coming in to tell you what I found." With that, he clicked off and Essie was befuddled and excited all at the same time. She looked at the bottom of the phone, which told her the time. *Portia's horses!* she thought, *why do I even need my wristwatch any more?* Her new smart phone told her the time, woke her up in the morning like an alarm clock, and answered any question she might have. How in the world did she ever get along without it? She gave the little device a friendly pat and placed it back in her pocket.

Within minutes, Ned was at her door, knocking and then entering without even waiting for a reply.

"Grandma!" he cried, coming over to her and sliding down on the sofa next to her. "What a day! I can't believe how everything fell into place. Boy, do I love being a detective. It's so exciting!"

"Okay, Sherlock," said Essie, attempting to calm down her grandson, "one thing at a time. Just take a deep breath, and then tell me all about it."

"I was interviewed by James Mills," said Ned. "I think he's the oldest son. He introduced himself as the CEO of Mills Electronics. He never mentioned Lester, or that Lester was the *actual* CEO, which is how the company is listed online."

"Maybe he just said that because his father is incapacitated," suggested Essie.

"You'd think he would at least have said his father was in the hospital and he was just standing in for him," argued Ned, "but no! James introduced himself as the CEO of Mills Electronics and—get this—he said they'd just gotten a major government contract and were expanding their computer division and needed to hire programmers—like me—asap. I mean, if I wanted to, I could probably get a really good job there. Too bad I like my present job."

"Yes," said Essie, "and also, I doubt you'd want to go to work for a potential murderer."

"That too," said Ned. "Anyway, I asked about the government contract, and he said it was very hush-hush, but that it was a military contract and involved weaponry and asked me if I'd be comfortable with that. I tried to get him to tell me more but he was pretty stubborn. He basically turned my questions around and quizzed me about my background and knowledge. I must have done well as he offered me a job on the spot."

"It sounds like you arrived there at just the right moment," observed Essie.

"It does," replied Ned. "I got a sense that all of this––the military contract, the weaponry, etc.—had just happened. There was really an air of excitement in the building. As I walked around the hallways, I observed employees talking among themselves excitedly. But that's not all. When I left, the secretary who walked me out and guided me back to the parking lot—it's a very complex facility and I needed help in finding my way out—chatted with me and I asked her about James Mills and how long he'd been CEO and she immediately told me that he'd just recently taken over since his father Lester had retired. I asked how recently, and she said just a matter of weeks."

"So, it sounds like Lester was actually running the company until right when he came to live here at Happy Haven," mused Essie. "Lester told us that he'd moved into Happy Haven a few weeks ago."

"I think so," said Ned. "I tried to get the secretary to tell me how she felt about either James or his father, but no go there. She was very discreet from there on."

"It doesn't matter, Ned," said Essie. "You did an amazing job. And you should know that what you found out today at the company reflects what I found out online. While you were there, I was searching for more information on Mills Electronics and Lester. I discovered an article that mentions that Mills has been offered a military contract to produce a mini-drone rocket, which supports what James Mills told you."

"Grandma," said Ned, "it's obviously not a coincidence that Lester Mills was hit by a rocket from a drone and that his own firm was just granted a contract from the Pentagon to produce a mini-drone rocket."

"Not in my book," agreed Essie. "And I can't think of a single scenario where Lester Mills would plan to have a drone rocket attack himself. I mean, if the man had wanted to commit suicide, there are many simpler ways to do it. And I met him, and he didn't seem at all despondent."

"No, it certainly seems as if his children are trying to kill him. But why?"

"That's what we have to find out," said Essie.

Chapter 23

After Ned left, Essie continued to research the Mills family online. Unfortunately, there wasn't much. She found some articles in the local Reardon newspapers about some social events the children had attended. All three were apparently still single and in their thirties. Essie figured that these facts alone probably bonded them together more than most siblings. The oldest son––the one who'd interviewed Ned—was James. Obviously, he was now running the company in his father's absence. But was his position one that had been given to him willingly by a grateful father, or was it one of necessity, born from the sudden incapacitation of the company's leader? The second son, Joseph, was only a year younger than his older brother. The daughter, Julie, was the baby, so to speak, two years younger than James. Essie mused that Lester Mills and his wife must have been very busy with three children so close together in age. Also, she found that Lester was presently 87 which meant he was in his fifties when his children were young.

She discussed these issues with her friends at dinner and told them about her recent discoveries and Ned's undercover operation at Mills Engineering. Opal had been, as expected, shocked that Essie had taken such drastic measures. Marjorie, on the other hand, had applauded Essie's initiative. Fay had remained neutral, always the peacemaker.

After dinner, Essie was relaxing in her recliner back in her apartment, playing with some of the amazing features on her new smart phone. She discovered that it would play music and even talk to her. All of a sudden, her door was opened abruptly and her daughter Claudia stormed in.

"Mom!" cried Essie's youngest, "what in the world has gotten into you?" She placed herself directly in front of Essie's chair, hands on her hips.

"Claudia," said Essie sweetly, quietly tucking her smart phone back in her pocket, "what brings you here?" She attempted to pull herself up from her chair, but Claudia bent over her, hands on the arm rests, preventing her from rising.

"I know what you're up to!" Claudia growled. "You think you're going to enlist Ned in this new quest of yours. Forcing him to go out there where those people make those incendiary devices. The ones that put your poor neighbor in the hospital and almost killed you! What were you thinking?" She threw her hands in the air and paced over to the window.

"Ned was never near any fireworks, Claudia," said Essie, defending herself. She tried to pull herself out of her chair, using her walker for balance.

"This is obviously a dangerous situation, Mom!" cried Essie's daughter, walking back and forth in the middle of Essie's small living room. "After all, the police have been investigating it. You told me so yourself."

Essie berated herself for revealing this information to her overly protective daughter under her breath. Obviously, the less Claudia knew about Essie's plans the better. "Oh, dear, they were just asking us questions about that firecracker that went astray. You know, did we see it? What did it look like? That sort of thing."

"That's not what you said, Mom," replied Claudia, and, coming back to her mother, and stabbing her finger in the air, "and that's not what Ned said."

"What did Ned say?" asked Essie cautiously. *Now why would her grandson tell her easily-riled up daughter anything?*

"He told *me* that he went out to Mills Electronics to spy on them!" she yelled, throwing her hands in the air. "Now, that has all the markings of one of your schemes, Mom! Spying! Of all the crazy ideas. It's one thing for you to go gallivanting around getting into trouble, but you leave my son out of it!" She shook her finger at Essie so hard, Essie almost tumbled back into her recliner.

"Actually, dear, the undercover idea was Ned's . . ."

"I don't care if it was J. Edgar Hoover's idea! Do not involve my poor son in these wild plots of yours!" Claudia had obviously so exhausted herself from pacing, yelling, and fretting, that she suddenly sank back onto Essie's comfortable sofa.

"Oh, Claudia," said Essie calmly, pushing her walker over to her daughter who was now softly sobbing. "I really think you're overreacting. All Ned did was go out and interview for a job that was listed on the Mills Electronics' website. He was even offered the job, he did so well on the interview."

"Of course he was offered the job," replied Claudia, mellowing a bit, "he's an amazing young man. He could get any job he went after."

"See," said Essie, giving her daughter a tender pat on the shoulder, "there's nothing to worry about." She sat down beside Claudia. "You're worried about nothing."

"I doubt that," sneered Claudia, "knowing you."

Just then, Essie's smart phone rang in her pocket. Essie tried to push the off button to send the call to voice mail like Ned had taught her, all the while smiling innocently at her daughter.

"What's that?" asked Claudia.

"Oh, nothing," said Essie, her ruse totally blown. Claudia reached over her mother's lap and into the pocket of her trousers, bringing out her smart phone.

"What's this, Mom?"

"It's one of those new smart phones, dear," replied Essie sweetly.

"And where did you get this?" asked Claudia. "I thought we just got you accustomed to your answering machine. You didn't even like it. It was—if I recall your words—too technical? If you think an answering machine is too technical, what do think a smart phone is?"

"Actually, dear," said Essie, "I'm finding it rather helpful. It does all sorts of things. Why, did you know it plays music . . . and it reminds me when to take my pills . . ."

"You have nurses who come in to give you your pills," said Claudia wisely. "You don't need a pill reminder."

"It talks to me," added Essie. "That's nice sometimes when I'm lonely."

"Lonely?" cried Claudia. "You? Lonely? You're the most outgoing person here at Happy Haven, I'd venture a guess. You talk to the garbage men. Mom, you're avoiding the question. Why do you have a smart phone. . . and . . . where did you get it?"

"I . . . .I . . . well," stammered Essie. "I need it for research."

"Research?" cried Claudia, shaking her head. "Why does a ninety-year-old lady in a retirement home need to do research?"

"Well, I do," said Essie defiantly. "I have my mysteries I need to solve and a smart phone allows me to search the Internet."

"You? Search the Internet?"

"Yes, dear," replied Essie. "You'd be surprised what I've discovered about Mr. Mills and his company on the Internet—and about his children."

"His children?" asked Claudia. "What do his children have to do with anything?"

"Maybe a lot," replied Essie. "That's why Ned needed to go . . . oh, never mind . . ."

"No, finish what you were about to say. Where did Ned go?" said Claudia, grabbing Essie's arm, "Did you send Ned over to—that Mills Electronics?"

"We, that is, Ned and I, suspect that Lester's, that is, Mr. Mills' children, may be involved in the accident that happened to their father on the Fourth of July. That's why . . ." She stopped abruptly, realizing that any further explanation would only solidify Claudia's fury at her for involving Ned in her plan.

"So you think his children had something to do with his accident? Why he's in the hospital?" Claudia asked.

"Possibly."

"And you sent Ned over there to investigate! Where a bunch of potential murderers work?" she screamed. "Are you crazy?"

"Now, Claudia, I thought we settled this . . ."

At that moment, Essie's door opened again. This time, Ned entered quickly and quietly and swiftly shut the door.

"Mom! For heaven's sake!" said the young man, coming over to the two women. "I could hear you screaming all the way down the hall. Calm down. And for the record, Grandma did not *send* me to Mills Electronics. The undercover plan was all mine. So blame me if you want to, not Grandma."

"All right," said Claudia, "but I bet she didn't try to talk you out of it."

"She couldn't have if she wanted to," replied Ned. "And I was never in danger. I was only there to ostensibly interview for a job—which I aced by the way. It just so happened that along the way, I found out some information about Mills Electronics and the Mills children that Grandma and I think will help solve the mystery . . ."

"Which is?"

"It's complicated, Mom," said Ned, "and I think once Grandma and I put it all together, we need to take it to the detectives on the case first."

"Oh, I get it. *You* bought her the smart phone. Didn't you?" Claudia's eyes widened, staring at her son. "Why would you do that? We'd just adjusted her to the answering machine."

"I'm right here," said Essie as her daughter and grandson argued about her. Essie's head moved back and forth from mother to son as they yelled their comments.

"She doesn't like the answering machine, Mom," stated Ned. "And she loves the smart phone. It helps her solve her mysteries. Plus, she can take it with her, so if you want to call her, you can get her, even if she's not in her apartment." Essie cringed when she heard Ned give Claudia this explanation.

"She can also send my calls to voice mail," replied Claudia. "That's what she just tried to do a few minutes ago when the smart phone rang. "Mom, you don't need a smart phone; you're smart enough."

"No, I *need* a smart phone because I *am* smart, Claudia," explained Essie with a grin. "Ned, we never asked why you were here."

"Grandma," said Ned, "I figured this was going to happen when I told Mom about my excursion to Mills Electronics. That was a huge mistake. I'm sorry. She immediately blamed you for getting me mixed up in this, and she stormed out of the house before I could explain that our undercover plan was all my idea."

"Claudia," said Essie, "can we all just calm down? Ned is fine. I'm fine. Nothing bad happened to anyone at Mills Electronics. The only person suffering is Mr. Mills and he's being cared for in the hospital."

"And I say let's keep it that way," argued Claudia. "Both of you! No more sleuthing! The last thing I need or want is for my mother or my son to be hurt or— arrested—because they're sticking their noses in something that doesn't concern them. And that's all I'm going to say now because Paul will be wondering where I am." With that, she grabbed her purse and headed out of Essie's room, leaving grandmother and grandson alone.

"I hope you aren't going to give up on our plans just because mom gives you a tongue lashing, Grandma," said Ned.

"Not me," replied Essie. "How about you?"

"No way," said Ned. "While I'm here, maybe we can go over a new idea I have."

"What is it? Another undercover plan?"

"I've been doing some additional investigating of Mills' daughter. She's single. She's actually a bit older than me, but most people think I act old for my age, so I thought I might just track her down and see if I can accidentally make her acquaintance at a bar or a pub."

"Ned, you rascal!" cried Essie. "That's a good idea. Do you think she frequents bars or clubs?"

"I guess she might from some things that the Mills' secretary mentioned to me when I went for the job interview. She made it sound as if Julie Mills is quite socially active, if you get my drift."

"Yes, we did discover that all three of the children are single, but we don't really know anything about their personal lives."

"We soon may," said Ned, nodding. "We soon may."

"But be careful, Ned," warned Essie. "If she was involved in her father's accident, then she wouldn't hesitate to hurt you if she suspected that you were trying to find out evidence about her."

"I know, Grandma. Don't worry. I'll be careful. After all, if I'm not, Mom will be all over you."

"That's true," said Essie, slyly. "Well, go get her, Romeo!"

"Grandma," said Ned, "you're embarrassing me."

"It's just reconnaissance, Ned," replied Essie. "Don't do anything risky."

"Sounds like a plan, Grandma," answered Ned. "Well, I'd better get going. If I stay here too long, you know what Mom will say."

"I do," said Essie. "And Ned, thanks for the smart phone. I love it!"

With that, Essie pulled her new device from her pocket and showed Ned. Ned gave Essie a quick hug and was then out the door.

Chapter 24

Tucking her phone back in her pocket and after a super quick potty break, Essie was soon on her way to dinner. Passing through the lobby, she couldn't help but notice Fay in her wheelchair in a secluded corner with Felix Federico. The dashing manager and Essie's tablemate were having a rather intense tête-à-tête, totally oblivious of anyone else. Essie perked up her ears to try to catch a piece of their conversation (although truth be told, it was, of course, a very one-sided conversation, with Felix doing all the talking).

Unfortunately, she couldn't hear a word and finally had to continue on her way to the dining room or else be revealed for the snoop that she was. Inside the dining room, she noticed that Marjorie and Opal were already seated at their table. Essie pushed her walker quickly over to her friends and parked her vehicle beside her regular chair.

"Opal," she said, "you left Fay out in the lobby."

"Oh, I didn't *leave* her there, Essie," replied Opal, nose tilted definitely upward. "She chose to remain there so she could be romanced by our leader, Senor Felix."

"Yes," confirmed Marjorie from Essie's other side, "you should have seen them going at it when we left."

"Going at it?" asked Essie. "Marjorie, you make them sound like a pair of rabbits."

"Who knows what that Felix has in mind," suggested Opal with a raised eyebrow. "I'm afraid he might be trying to take advantage of dear, sweet Fay."

"Oh, bag of shag!" huffed Essie, "I have faith in Fay. She may be quiet but she's not one to let some man bully her about. She's just enjoying having a handsome man flirt with her."

"But why?" asked Marjorie, obviously deflated. "Why is he taking such an interest in Fay? She's decades older and she can't even talk to him."

"Maybe that's part of her charm," observed Essie. "My John always told me that I was my loveliest when I was asleep. At the time, I thought he meant I looked like Sleeping Beauty. Only recently, did I realize that he probably meant that when I was sleeping I wasn't talking."

"No," argued Opal, "there's something more to it. Felix seems genuinely interested in Fay—more so than any of the other ladies here at Happy Haven."

"Shh!" cried Marjorie suddenly. "He's bringing her back." And as all three women turned and looked where Marjorie was nodding, they indeed did see that Felix Federico, manager of Happy Haven, was pushing Fay towards their table. Both Felix and Fay bore huge smiles.

"Whatever they were discussing," said Essie, "must have been very stimulating."

"Fay!" cried Opal, as Felix parked Fay at her regular dining spot. As he bent down, a lock of curly black hair fell seductively over his forehead. "We wondered if you were going to join us for dinner."

"Oh, I would not let this lovely lady miss her meal," declared Felix. "And how are all of you tonight?" He smiled at them, his mouthful of gleaming white teeth sparkling.

"We've missed you, Felix," said Marjorie, nudging her shoulder suggestively against the man's arm. "You seem to be spending all your time with Fay lately . . ."

"Oh, I'm sure you charming ladies do not begrudge your friend Fay the little extra time that I spend with her?" he questioned with a smile. The ladies, of course, returned his smile. "Someone needs to give Miss Fay some extra attention, don't you think? She is so special." At this, he bent down and kissed Fay's cheek. Fay squealed and giggled and the other three ladies looked aghast. "Now then," he continued without missing a beat, "kisses all around!" He lifted Fay's hand and gave it a short peck. Then he moved around the table and bestowed hand kisses on all of the remaining women. "Have a wonderful dinner, lovely ladies!" he said, as he moved on to the next table, where the ladies there had their hands (and some, their cheeks) ready for some Felix lips.

"So," began Essie, as soon as Felix was out of ear range, "what was that all about?"

"I don't know," swooned Marjorie, "but I hope he makes the rounds and comes back to our table."

"If that man spends as much time actually managing Happy Haven as he does romancing the female residents, it must be in very good shape," added Opal.

"No," said Essie, "not the hand kissing stuff. That's just his style. You know, he's Mexican or Brazilian or something . . ."

"Essie, you can't say that," cried Marjorie. "That's prejudiced."

"I don't know one American man who has ever kissed my hand, Marjorie, and neither do you. I'm not prejudiced; I'm just observant."

"I mean we don't know where Felix is from; he might be from Poughkeepsie for all we know."

"That kiss didn't feel like a Poughkeepsie kiss," observed Opal.

"And what does a Poughkeepsie kiss feel like, Ms. Worldly Wise?" asked Marjorie.

"He's not from Poughkeepsie," cried Essie. "You all are being ridiculous. He's from some Latin country. But that's not the point. He uses his charm on us to manipulate us and . . ."

"And he can manipulate me all he wants . . ." added Marjorie, leaning back in her chair, eyes closed.

Santos arrived to collect their dinner orders.

"Santos," said Essie to their young server, "you're Mexican. What nationality is Felix Federico? Can you tell by his accent? Have you discussed him with your colleagues back in the kitchen?"

"Oh, Miss Essie," said Santos, picking up Essie's dinner menu which she had checked with her choice of entree and vegetable, "nobody knows. But it is not just an accent; he is fluent in Spanish. I have tried to listen to him speak because sometimes it is easier to see where might be his home when he speak Spanish, you know?"

"And?" asked Essie.

"No one in kitchen know for sure. Señor Federico not talk about himself. But he very nice to us in kitchen."

"Hmm," said Essie. "Is he especially nice to the female employees?"

"I not know what you mean, Miss Essie," said Santos, puzzled. By now, he had collected all four menu orders and was on his way to the next table.

"Give it up, Essie," said Marjorie when Santos had moved on. "There's nothing there. Felix is simply a nice man who is polite and charming with the ladies. Why he has glommed onto Fay may be something we'll never understand, but it certainly doesn't seem to be bothering Fay, and I don't think we need to be worried." Essie looked over at Fay who was smiling the same sweet smile she always wore. Indeed, if anything, Felix Federico's attention to their special tablemate had only made Fay happier. Even so, Essie was curious. Maybe not worried, but definitely curious.

"So, Essie," began Opal, "I was just telling Marjorie before you arrived that I called the hospital a bit ago and they reported that Lester's condition is unchanged. I guess that means that he's still unconscious and in a coma."

"I'm glad to hear that he's remaining stable," replied Essie. "And I have to report to you all, that my grandson Ned and I have discovered some new clues about the rocket that hit him. Look at this." She reached into her pocket and brought out her new smartphone.

"Oh my!" cried Opal. "That's one of those smart telephones, isn't it?"

"Yes!" said Essie. "My grandson Ned got it for me to do my sleuthing. I've already figured out a lot of what it can do. It can play music and talk to me and be an alarm clock—and a lot more. I can conduct my research on it too. Look!" Essie showed the women the little screen and how she could insert search terms and bring up information from the Internet.

"That's amazing!" cried Marjorie.

"It is," agreed Essie. "Ned and I found out some amazing things too about Lester and Mills Electronics. It seems that the company has recently been offered a government contract to build drone-operated rockets for the military."

"What?" cried Opal. "You mean Lester's company is manufacturing the very device that hit him?"

"Not yet," declared Essie, "The contract is new. Ned and I aren't sure if they've started production. . ."

"But they must have prototypes in development," suggested Marjorie, "if they've gotten a contract."

"We don't know that either," replied Essie, "but Ned went out there . . ."

"To Mills Electronics?" asked Opal.

"Yes," said Essie, in a whisper. "It was an undercover operation."

"Essie! Undercover!" cried Marjorie. "That's dangerous. Your grandson is so young. That might not be safe."

"He was very careful," said Essie. "Actually, there was a job opening listed on the Mills Electronics website that Ned was qualified for, so he went out there and applied. They even offered it to him, but he already has a job. Anyway, while he was there, he was able to do a lot of snooping."

Santos arrived with their entrees and placed a plate in front of each lady.

"Yum!" declared Marjorie, and the other women followed suit. Soon, they were all four digging into their meals, Essie's tale of Ned's bravado put on hold while appetites were sated. When they'd finished scooping into their dinners, the discussion continued.

"So, Essie," asked Opal, "was Ned able to find anything at Mills Electronics?"

"He actually met with James Mills—he's Lester's oldest son—and presently the CEO of the company. James interviewed Ned for the job and he's the one who offered the job to Ned."

"Essie, if Ned took that job, he'd be able to really get an inside view of what's going on at Mills Electronics," offered Marjorie.

"Yes," agreed Essie, "but I can't ask him to do that. As it is, he was able to find out a lot just by talking to one of the secretaries there. Evidently, the oldest son James is running the place since Lester left. Ned found that all three children—James, Joseph, and Julie—are very social and he also found out where they like to hang out. Ned is going to go check out some clubs where the daughter Julie frequents and see if he can strike up a conversation with her."

"Oh, Essie, that sounds really dangerous," said Opal, "especially if the children are involved in the attack on Lester."

"Well, at the moment," said Essie, "it doesn't appear that the police think the children are involved, or at least they haven't made any moves to arrest them. Somebody needs to stir things up with those kids if we want to find out what's going on. Ned thinks he can find out information from this Julie and I trust that Ned is clever enough to do so without endangering himself."

Essie glanced over at Fay who was trying to manipulate a spoonful of sauce into her mouth. Her attention seemed to be waning and her eyes wandered off, causing the gravy to dribble over the bowl of the spoon and down her chin. Fay seemed oblivious.

"Oh, Fay!" cried Opal, reaching over and patting her friend's face with her napkin. "You need to pay more attention to what you're doing."

"She's probably dreaming about Felix," said Marjorie.

"She's dreaming he's whispering sweet nothings in her ear again and holding her hand and kissing her cheek," said Essie wryly.

Fay, however, ignored her friends with a smile and continued to slurp the gravy into her mouth. Suddenly, she looked at Opal and pushed her hand away, daintily lifting her own napkin to her lips and patting them.

"My, my!" declared Marjorie, "Fay, I didn't know you to be so proper."

Fay giggled at Marjorie and the entire table joined in.

Essie observed her chubby friend in her wheelchair and said, "Sometimes I think she knows exactly what she's doing and sometimes I don't. I just wish she'd say something once in a while, so we'd all know what's going on in that head of hers."

"Well, we know one for certain," said Opal. "Something is going on." The four women all stared at Fay, and Fay just smiled blissfully back.

Chapter 25

As the four pals were chatting on their way out of the dining hall, they failed to see the entrance of the two detectives—Blake and Farley—who'd just arrived through the main door. However, the detectives noticed them and immediately walked over to them.

"Ladies," said Blake, in his robust manly voice. The four women immediately turned.

"Oh, Detective Blake," said Essie, somewhat aflutter as she was not expecting to see these two individuals again so soon. Opal and Marjorie remained quiet and allowed Essie to do the talking for them.

"Might we have a word with you all?" Blake asked softly, gesturing to some empty chairs off to one side of the spacious Happy Haven lobby. The ladies nodded and wandered over to the furniture grouping, Opal pushing Fay's wheelchair. Blake and Farley followed them and pulled up two straight back chairs so they could sit close to the women.

"We felt you ladies should know of something that has happened in case it got reported in the news," began Farley, softly.

"Oh, no!" cried Opal. "Is it Lester? Is he worse?"

"Ma'am," said Blake, "he's fine—now. However, earlier this evening there was an attempt on his life."

"What?" cried Opal, "What do you mean?"

"It appears," said the woman detective Farley, "that someone pulled the plug on the electrical equipment in Mr. Mills' room that maintained his IV medications. Luckily, this set off an alarm and the head nurse reached Mr. Mills and reattached the equipment before Mr. Mills was adversely affected. But she called us right away and we called in our forensics unit. They brushed for fingerprints, and it looks as if someone did this deliberately. It wasn't an accident."

"Oh, poor Lester!" cried Opal, tugging at her necklace and sobbing. Fay reached over and patted Opal's shoulder gently.

"I knew it," declared Essie. "They were just trying to finish off the job."

"What do you mean, Miss Essie?" asked Farley. "Who is *they*?"

"Lester Mills' children. We've tried to tell you," Essie said. "I'm sure they were behind it—and I'm sure they were behind the rocket attack that put their father in the hospital in the first place."

"Miss Essie," said Blake, "we've interviewed all three of Mills' children and none of them have any motive to hurt their father. We've checked with the employees at Mills Electronics and family friends and it appears that the Mills family was a happy one—no animosity between father and children."

"Well, you didn't investigate thoroughly enough," said Essie. "What about that earring I gave you? The one Marjorie and I found out in the field where the rocket was shot from?"

"We asked Miss Mills, and she didn't recognize the earring . . ." began Farley.

"Of course she'd say that," said Essie. "She wouldn't admit it was hers because then she'd have to explain why she was out in that field. But what about the photograph of her wearing the earring that's hanging in Mr. Mills' apartment? Just look at her in that picture and you'll see she's wearing the same earring."

"Actually, we went to his apartment to do just that, but we couldn't find any such photograph in his room," replied Blake.

"What?" cried Essie.

"Essie," said Marjorie, "the daughter probably took that photograph out of Lester's room as soon as the police showed her the earring—or maybe before. She must have known she was wearing it in the picture and knew she probably lost it in the field and if they found it, it would incriminate her. She's probably going to be incredibly careful now and really mad."

"Detective," said Essie, "we promise you we did see that photograph in Lester's room and his daughter was wearing that earring. You can believe it. Marjorie and I will swear to it. Won't we, Marjorie?"

"I will," agreed Marjorie. "If there's one thing I know, detectives, it's expensive jewelry, and that was a real ruby earring."

"I should have taken that photograph off the wall," mumbled Essie, "instead of leaving it there in Lester's room. What a doofus I am!"

"Don't blame yourself, Essie," urged Opal. "You had no idea that all this would happen—that Lester's children would try to kill him—"

"Now, ladies, we don't know that," began Blake. "The person or persons responsible for what has happened to Lester Mills could just as easily be a business rival. Mr. Mills' company is extremely successful."

"And we don't want you to do anything to endanger yourselves," added Farley. "Whoever it is, is dangerous and we don't want any of you to do anything else because you might get hurt. So please, let us do the investigating."

All of the ladies who could speak, immediately assured the detectives that they would be perfectly well-behaved and not risk their lives. The detectives apparently believed them and were soon on their way.

As soon as they were gone, Essie got the attention of her three table-mates.

"Those detectives are ignoring the obvious. I don't know why Lester Mills' children want to do him in, but it seems that they do—and we appear to be the only ones who realize it. We have to prove it, or the next time they try to kill him, they'll probably succeed!"

"Oh, no!" cried Opal. "Poor Lester!"

"Quit blubbering, Opal," demanded Essie. "This is no time for hysteria. We need to all work together to help Mr. Mills and protect him from those horrible children of his as he can't do it himself. We need to prove to the police that they're behind the attack on Lester."

"But how, Essie?" asked Marjorie.

"Maybe we should take turns sitting with Lester in his hospital room," offered Opal, "so that one of us is always there in case one of the children attempt to detach his medical equipment again . . ."

"That's ridiculous!" cried Essie, "We're four old women who live in a retirement home. How are we going to do that?"

"We could set up a schedule and each take taxis over to the hospital when it's our turn," suggested Opal.

"And which one of the four of us is going to take the night shift?" asked Essie. "And how long are we going to do this for? What if weeks go by and the police haven't solved the case? Are we supposed to sit by his side indefinitely? And do you actually think the hospital would *allow* any of us to do that? They'd report us to the police, and Detective Blake and Farley would come running over and force us to return home. You know it."

"So, what do you suggest?" asked Opal, her suggestion discounted.

"We have to figure out *why* the Mills children so desperately want their father dead," said Essie. "Blake and Farley just told us that they'd investigated the children and found no *obvious* motives, but we all know that there must be a motive. We have to dig deeper."

"Maybe your grandson could go back to Mills Electronics and snoop around some more," suggested Marjorie.

"No," answered Essie. "I've imposed on Ned enough. He has a job and that needs to be his top priority—not being his grandmother's sidekick. And besides, my daughter Claudia was all over my tushie earlier for getting her precious baby involved in one of my," and here Essie made air quotes, "hair-brained schemes."

"Maybe we should all go out to Mills Electronics and sleuth around," suggested Opal.

"I doubt we'd find anything more than Ned did," replied Essie, "and if a young man ostensibly applying for a job for which he was highly qualified can't infiltrate the place, how do you propose that four old ladies can?"

"Maybe Opal could go by herself," suggested Marjorie, "and claim she's Lester's secret lover and demand that the children take her in."

"Take her in where?" asked Essie. "Marjorie, that's ridiculous! Why should his children take in his lover, even if he had such a thing?"

"And I couldn't do that anyway," exclaimed Opal. "I could never pretend to be someone's lover."

"Do you object to the pretend part or the lover part?" queried Marjorie flippantly.

"Stop it, Marjorie!" said Essie. "This isn't helping."

"I wasn't trying to help; I was trying to get Opal's goat." Marjorie sighed deeply and slouched back in the sofa where she was lounging.

Essie looked around. Their lively conversation was attracting attention from some other residents sitting in the lobby. Essie gave her friends a meaningful glare and motioned them to sit closer together.

"Anyway," Essie began afresh, "I don't think we need to worry about Lester's safety as the police have a guard by his room now. What we need to focus on is finding some clue or evidence that will direct the police to Lester's children. I don't think going to the company headquarters would be feasible or productive for the four of us, and besides, Ned just tried that and I think he got all the information he could. No. We need to direct our attention to finding the *reason* Lester's children want him dead. There must be a motive. We need to put on our thinking caps and consider all the possibilities. What could it be?"

"Maybe Lester was a cruel disciplinarian when the children were young, and they've always wanted to turn the tables on him?" suggested Marjorie.

"I don't accept that!" countered Opal. "I know the man, remember. He was always so considerate and thoughtful. I can't imagine him as a mean parent. I just can't."

"Sometimes," said Marjorie, "people put on masks. Maybe Lester's really a terrible task-master and drove his children like some mad slave driver when they were young. They've waited all their lives to get back at him and now's their chance."

"Why now?" asked Essie. "Even considering your idea about Lester being this monster is correct . . ."

"Which he isn't," added Opal.

"What?" said Marjorie.

"Yes," said Essie. "Why now? Why all of a sudden would the children decide to do in the old man, so to speak? They've had years and years to *off* him. Why wait until he enters a retirement home? Surely, as old as he is, they could just wait until he dies naturally. They probably all inherit his estate, don't you think?"

"Maybe they just found out that Lester's leaving everything to Opal," offered Marjorie.

"That's ridiculous, Marjorie!" Opal cried. "I just saw the man for the first time a few days ago. He had no idea I even lived here at Happy Haven until the night of that flash dance. He didn't have any time to change his will—not that he'd do such a thing."

"I agree with Opal," said Essie. "I don't think Lester changed his will in favor of Opal. However, I'm not so sure that all of this might not have *something* to do with the man's will."

"How so?" asked Marjorie.

"If the children are trying to kill their father," argued Essie, "it appears to be motivated by something recent. What if that something is a *change* in Lester's will?"

"You mean he might have disinherited them or threatened to disinherit them?" asked Opal.

"It's a possibility," said Essie.

"Being cut out of a will might certainly motivate someone to consider murder," continued Essie. "But the question is why?"

"Why they would consider murder?" asked Opal.

"No," replied Essie, "why Lester would cut his children out of his will? Why now? What happened to make him change his mind? If that's what happened."

"It might be something that just the family knows about," suggested Marjorie. "And if so, that might be why the police can't find any motive."

"What would it be?" asked Opal.

"Maybe the children did something that antagonized Lester, and he found out recently and decided to cut them out of the will and they found out about it and have been trying to kill him—but trying to make it look accidental so they won't get blamed."

"This is all a huge amount of speculation, Essie," declared Opal, skeptically. She folded her arms and leaned back in her seat, chewing on her lip.

"I know, I know," said Essie with a sigh. "It's probably none of this, but it has to be something. Someone tried to kill Lester Mills. We know that. The police may chalk the rocket up as an accident, but that attack in the hospital was real and it's unlikely that *both* events are accidental. Someone wants Lester dead. Why? We don't know for sure. Who? We think the children but it might be someone else. How can find out? We can't question Lester. We can't feasibly question the children. What's left?"

"Nothing," replied Opal. "We're out of options."

"No we're not," said Essie. "I say we try one more time to search Lester' room. This time, much more thoroughly. The first time we had to leave suddenly and didn't really get to finish our search. I have the feeling we missed something."

Chapter 26

The second time around, they planned their search better. Essie managed to sneak the master key from right under Phyllis's eyes while she was chatting on the phone. Opal and Fay still remained the lookouts at the end of the hallway, and Essie and Marjorie did the actual looking. But this time, instead of Marjorie flipping through items in one room and Essie tossing a few things in another, the two women worked systematically together, starting at one end of the living room and examining every single item in Lester Mills' apartment. They pulled out dishes from his kitchen cupboards. They opened up cartons of food in his tiny refrigerator. They rolled up floor rugs and looked underneath them. Then, when they found nothing, they put everything back neatly. Luckily, Lester Mills' apartment was just as small as all of the apartments at Happy Haven and, being a relatively new resident, he didn't have all that many items in his dwelling. This made for a fairly quick search and by about a half-hour later, the two women had wound their way into the man's bedroom.

"Marjorie, Look!" cried Essie, entering the bedroom and pointing to the wall above the dresser.

"Look at what?" asked the pert redhead.

"The police are right," declared Essie. "The picture that had Lester's daughter in it wearing those ruby earrings like the one we found in the field is gone!"

"Oh, my, Essie," replied Marjorie, wandering over to the dresser and running her hand over the empty space on the wall where a lone nail marked the spot where a picture had once hung. "You're right."

"The daughter must have taken it down," cried Essie. "I knew I should have taken it with me the other day." She rolled her walker over to join Marjorie. "She's probably disposed of that picture by now. Oh, hairy bears! Now we really have to find something here to incriminate those children—otherwise I'm afraid they may get away with attempted murder."

"Well, get busy then, Essie," said Marjorie, pointing around the room at locations for Essie to check. The small bedroom provided little spots for additional clues. There was a single bed, the dresser, and a nightstand with a lamp. There were no throw rugs, just carpeting.

"Let's start with the dresser," announced Essie, as she opened the top left drawer. "Underwear. This is your domain, Marjorie. Have at it." Essie moved aside and gestured for Marjorie to investigate Lester Mills' unmentionables. Marjorie immediately reached in and pulled out a fistful of plain white tighty whities.

"In the underwear department," declared Marjorie, holding up the evidence, "Lester Mills is boring as cauliflower."

"I'll be sure to let Opal know," sneered Essie. "Keep going. Is there anything else in there?"

"T-shirts!" cried Marjorie with mock enthusiasm, as she pulled out a neat stack of folded white shirts.

The two women unfolded all of the items and, finding nothing, refolded them and placed them back in the dresser drawer. Then they continued on through the other five drawers. In one drawer, they discovered sweaters and in a third, two sets of pajamas. The remaining drawers were empty.

"He doesn't own much, does he?" asked Marjorie.

"He just moved in," said Essie in the absent man's defense. "Give him time."

"Let's look in his bathroom," suggested Marjorie. "I've heard that sometimes, people hide things in pill bottles or cosmetics containers if they really don't want someone to find something . . ."

"We'll get there," replied Essie. "Let's finish the bedroom first." There was nothing on top of the dresser, so the women continued on around to the bed. They pulled back the covers and looked in the pillow cases. "We should check under the mattress," offered Essie.

"I'm not lifting this mattress up, Essie," responded Marjorie in a huff.

"Oh, all right," Essie said. "I suppose the man wouldn't hide anything under the mattress because then he couldn't reach it either. What about under the bed?"

"Same problem," said Marjorie. "Can you imagine him on his hands and knees to shove something under his bed?"

"Look there anyway," demanded Essie, pointing to the floor.

"Why me?" asked Marjorie. "You look!"

"I use a walker," declared Essie. "I can't get on my hands and knees. Just do it. I know you're very limber and flexible—at least that's what you're always telling us at dinner . . ."

"Oh, all right," replied Marjorie, reluctantly crouching on her knees and peering under the bed. "There's nothing there. Not even any dust bunnies." She stood up with difficulty but attempted to make it look easier than it was for her.

"The nightstand," said Essie, opening the drawer on the small table. Inside, she found a magnifying glass and a box of tissues. "Not much here. I do like that he does the same crossword puzzles that I do." She picked up the paper-bound puzzle book beside the lamp on the nightstand and it fell open. "Oh, shady Sadie! Marjorie, look!" In between the pages of the crossword puzzle book rested an envelope.

"What's that?" asked Marjorie.

"Just my question," replied Essie, setting down the puzzle book and examining the envelope. "It's sealed and there's no address."

"Why would he put that there?" asked Marjorie. "Maybe it was something he wanted to remember to mail and this way he was sure he wouldn't forget to do it."

"Only one way to find out," replied Essie, applying her fingernail to the inside of the envelope flap. "I'm going to open it."

"Essie!" cried Marjorie. "You can't do that. It's like a federal crime to open someone's mail."

"This isn't mail, Marjorie," said Essie. "Just because it's an envelope doesn't mean it's mail. There's no address, no stamp, no return address—and most important—it's not in a mailbox."

"True," agreed Marjorie, "but it is sealed and it's in Lester Mills' apartment in his book. If he'd wanted you to open it, he'd have sent it to you."

"Don't quibble," Essie said. "We don't have time for that. This could be an important clue. It's obviously important to Lester otherwise why would he place it here where he could find it easily and why would he seal the envelope? I'm opening it." She ignored Marjorie's gasp and ripped the seal, opening the plain white envelope. Inside, there was one folded sheet of paper which she removed.

"What does it say?" asked Marjorie, her qualms forgotten.

"Addendum to the Will of Lester Mills," read Essie, "and it gives the date." Essie read down the page silently.

"What does it say, Essie?" demanded Marjorie, jumping up and down like a schoolgirl.

"It says all sorts of technical things, but the gist of it all appears to be that Lester Mills is disinheriting his children because of a disagreement he has with them over the direction they want to take the company. Apparently, Lester does not want to accept the government contract to build those military drones. The children do. Looks like the disagreement became so heated that he felt it necessary to remove them from the will . . ."

"But Essie," said Marjorie, "this addendum to Lester's will is here in his crossword puzzle book. Do you think his lawyer even knows about this?"

"Well, I doubt it, not with Lester lying unconscious in the hospital," said Essie.

"And as long as Lester's out of commission, the children can evidently sign any government contract they want."

"Can they?" asked Essie. "I would guess they have the authority while Lester is hospitalized, but they must know that he doesn't want this contract and as soon as he's conscious, he'll probably nullify it."

"Unless he doesn't *regain* consciousness." suggested Marjorie.

"Exactly," said Essie.

"We have to get this will addendum to the police right away," said Marjorie.

"I agree."

Suddenly, they heard the door to Lester's apartment open. The two women froze.

"Marjorie! Essie!" Opal's voice whispered out in a panicky manner. "Where are you?"

"Back here," whispered back Essie. Opal's head appeared in the bedroom doorway.

"Lester's children are heading down the hallway—fast!" she cried in a quiet voice. "I left Fay at the end of the hallway. I don't think we have time to get out without them seeing us."

Just then, the front door to the apartment opened again. Then, as soon as it opened, the door closed quietly again.

All three women looked at each other with dread. Essie set the crossword puzzle book back on the nightstand and stuck the will addendum back in the envelope and the envelope deep inside the basket of her walker. Then she motioned for the other two women to quietly follow her into Lester's large walk-in closet. Being as how all of the apartments at Happy Haven had basically the same layout, they all knew what the inside of the closet looked like. As Lester had only recently moved in, the three women scooted down to the far end and cuddled up together. It was impossible for them to actually hide from anyone who might look into the closet as it had no door, but they were hoping that whoever had entered the apartment would not come into the bedroom.

"Essie," whispered Opal, "if they come into the bedroom and look into the closet, they'll find us."

"Then you'd better hope they don't look in the closet, Opal."

"What took you so long?" demanded Opal.

"That's your concern now?" replied Essie.

"Quiet, both of you," said Marjorie, shh-ing her friends and trying to hide her small body behind one of Lester's overcoats that was hanging down in front of her.

"I can't just leave Fay sitting alone out there in the hallway," whispered Opal.

"Be quiet, Opal," responded Essie, trying to grab a portion of the coat that was hiding Marjorie. "We may be just of the verge of being murdered. I'm sure *our* situation is much more grave than Fay's. She's just sitting out in the hallway. I'm sure someone will take pity on her eventually and drive her back to her room."

"But Lester's children will pass her in the hallway," cried Opal, obviously more worried about her friend than herself.

"So?" questioned Essie. "Fay can take care of herself. Just what do you think they're going to do to her in the hallway?"

"Maybe we should just go out there and claim we entered the wrong room by mistake," suggested Marjorie.

"If we did that," said Essie, "then why are we hiding in the closet?"

"Don't you have your new smart phone with you, Essie?" asked Marjorie. "Call somebody."

"Who?" asked Essie. "And tell them what? That the three of us are hiding in a closet in an apartment that we *broke* into? No. We're better off just hiding and hope they leave."

"Essie, sometimes you are just too smart for your own good," said Opal.

Essie shrugged and pulled the overcoat further around her body. Marjorie grabbed the coat, pulling it away from Essie. Then Opal grabbed a corner of it, pulling it away from the other two. All three women shivered noticeably as footsteps could be heard in the adjoining room.

Chapter 27

"Where did you hide it, Dad?" they heard a female voice say from the living room. This question was followed by the sound of items being moved or tossed. The woman in the living room stomped around, flinging things all over the place, in her attempt to find something.

As the sounds came closer to the bedroom, the three ladies clutched each other and squeezed their bodies closer together. If the woman—they assumed it was Lester's daughter Julie—came into the bedroom, she couldn't help but notice the three of them huddled together at the end of Lester's large closet.

All of a sudden, the sound of Lester's front door opening could be heard again. A man's voice whispered out, "Julie, you need to get out now! Those two detectives just came in the front entrance. I think they're looking for the manager to let them into Dad's place!"

"Great," replied the woman's voice with a major tone of annoyance. "I just got started."

"I take it you didn't find it?" asked the male voice.

"What do you think?" replied the female voice, followed by more sounds of things being knocked over and moved.

"Come on," said the male voice with greater urgency. "Hurry!"

"Oh, all right!" said the female voice.

The three ladies in the closet heard the distinct click of the front door. They waited for a few seconds but it appeared that the two people in the living room had truly departed.

"Come on," cried Essie to her companions. "Let's get going. We can't be here when those detectives get here."

Essie used her walker to pull herself up from the closet floor. Marjorie and Opal also grabbed onto the sides of Essie's ride to assist them in standing. Once all three were upright, Essie shoved her vehicle quickly out of the bedroom closet and cautiously into the small hallway to the living room. She looked around carefully to be certain that no one remained to jump them. Seeing that the apartment was truly empty, she wheeled herself into the living room and over to the main entrance. Here she carefully but quickly opened the front door and gingerly poked her head out.

"No one's visible yet," she announced, gesturing for Marjorie and Opal to follow her out of Lester Mills' apartment. Once outside, Essie quickly locked Lester's door with the stolen master key and then made a beeline down the hallway where the women could see Fay sitting calmly in her wheelchair at the intersection. When they reached their friend, Opal apologized profusely to Fay, grabbed the handles of the wheelchair and all four of them hustled down the hallway to the elevator which had just arrived—luckily empty—on the second floor. They quickly scooted inside.

Essie said, "We all need to go to my room and read this thing." She patted the basket on her walker.

"What thing?" asked Opal.

"We'll explain when we get there," said Marjorie.

"First," said Essie, "I have to return Phyllis's master key. You three divert her attention at the front desk while I replace it."

"Now how are we supposed to do that?" asked Opal. "I'm not used to these illegal activities, Essie. I have lived a particularly moral life."

"And you may go on doing so, Opal," declared Essie. "Just distract the woman for a few seconds. Yuppy's guppies! Tell her you like her hair or something."

You mean lie," said Marjorie. "I can do that."

The elevator door opened with a ding and Essie stormed out in the lead and over to the front desk. Luckily, the detectives and Felix were nowhere in sight at the moment. Phyllis was presently talking to someone on the telephone and it sounded like a potential resident.

"Yes, ma'am," said their receptionist, "it's a lovely facility. We have all sorts of activities for our residents. And our chef is fabulous." Marjorie took her cue from this overheard snippet of conversation and plopped herself in front of Phyllis.

"Tell her about the chicken pies," said Marjorie to Phyllis to keep her from glancing over at Essie. Opal scooted Fay over to stand next to them. Meanwhile, Essie snuck to the far end of the front desk where the master keys hung on a board. She reached into her pocket and removed the gold key with the tag on a string and leaned over and hung it on an empty nail. Then she quickly joined the other ladies, smiling and giving them a subtle gesture to indicate she was ready to go.

"Oh, here's one of our residents now," said Phyllis into the receiver. "Maybe you'd like to talk to her. . ." Phyllis started to hand the phone to Marjorie, but Essie had already started out of the lobby and down her hallway followed by the three other ladies. Phyllis shook her head, mystified by the sudden appearance and then disappearance of the foursome.

Essie rolled down her hallway, arriving at her doorway and ushering her compatriots into her apartment. Once inside, all except Fay collapsed onto the closest sofa or arm chair. Essie pulled her walker next to her recliner and dropped down into its comfortable depths.

"All right, Essie," demanded Opal. "Now, what did you find? I hope that all this subterfuge has been for something."

"Tea first," ordered Marjorie.

"You want tea, Marjorie?" asked Essie, "then you fix it yourself." Marjorie gave a huff, pulled herself out of the sofa, and headed over to Essie's stove where she filled the kettle with water from the sink. She got down Essie's tea box from the cupboard and brought it over to the coffee table.

"Make your choices," she said, returning quickly with tea cups and saucers for all four ladies.

"I'm waiting, Essie," demanded Opal. "What on earth did you find?"

"Just this," declared Essie, reaching into the basket of her nearby walker and bringing out the white envelope.

"And what is that?" asked Opal.

"It appears to be an addition to Lester Mills' will!" she announced.

In a few minutes, the water was boiling on the stove and Marjorie brought the kettle around and filled each woman's cup. Then she returned the kettle to the stove and joined the group.

"Read it, Essie," encouraged Marjorie.

"Yes, Essie, read it. As it appears we all risked our lives to get it," added Opal.

"Here goes," said Essie, lifting the flap on the envelope and bringing out the folded piece of paper. She unfolded it and began to read, "Codicil to the Last

Will and Testament of Lester Earl Mills. I, Lester Earl Mills, being of sound mind, declare this to be the final codicil to my last will and testament which was executed by me on January 3, 2009. In addition to the original document, I am adding the following provision: All monies and properties to be inherited by any/all of my children shall be forfeited by them if, in their capacity as officers of said company, they contract with any agency/ies connected to the United States military or involved in any military support function."

"That's it?" asked Marjorie.

"That's it," said Essie, turning the codicil over in an attempt to see if any other information might be written on the back.

"Opal," said Essie, "you're the one with the legal and business background. Just what does this mean?"

"It seems fairly straightforward, Essie," said Opal, taking the paper from Essie and reviewing the short paragraph herself. "It seems that Lester doesn't want his company contracting with the military and he's gone so far as to put it in his will."

"To make certain that his children follow his wishes, even after he's gone," added Marjorie.

"That seems pretty drastic," said Essie. "Can he even do that? I mean, once he hands the company over to the children, shouldn't they be the ones making the decisions?"

"You mean shouldn't his children—the ones we think are trying to kill him—be making decisions for the company?" asked Opal.

"Is it fair for him to run the company after he's gone?" asked Marjorie.

"It's his company!" cried Opal. "If his children don't like how he runs it, they can go elsewhere and start their own company."

"Stop!" cried Essie. "None of this is for us to judge. We don't know Lester's reasons for making this codicil. He might have very good reasons."

"And he might not," said Marjorie.

"But whatever," continued Essie, "this codicil certainly does seem to be sufficient motive for murder."

"I bet that's what the daughter was looking for when she was hunting in Lester's living room while we were stuck in that closet," said Opal.

"Of course it was," agreed Marjorie. "Lester probably told his children about the codicil to threaten them to keep them from signing the contract with the military but didn't tell them where it was. Or they guessed he'd drawn it up but didn't know where it was."

"The logical thing was for Lester to file it with his lawyer, not hide it in his crossword puzzle book," said Essie. "Why didn't he do that?"

"I'm guessing that it just all happened so fast," suggested Marjorie. "Maybe he'd just decided to do this a day or so ago and hadn't had time to get it to his lawyer."

"Or even mention it to his lawyer . . ." added Opal.

"That's why the children were so desperate," said Essie. "They had to do away with their father before he filed this new codicil if they wanted to sign this military contract. Once Lester filed the addendum with his lawyer, it would become common knowledge and it would be unlikely that the military would proceed with a contract with Mills Electronic."

"I guess the children must have figured that that drone rocket that struck Lester would just be thought to be a stray firecracker from the city display. I mean it *was* the Fourth of July. They didn't think through their plan very well, did they?" said Marjorie.

"I guess they had so much faith in that drone of theirs that they felt invincible," replied Essie.

"So who's running Mills Electronics?" asked Opal, "Lester or his children?"

"We don't know," said Essie. "It sounds like Lester is still the titular head even though he's retired and living here at Happy Haven, but the children run things on a daily basis."

"I wonder why Lester didn't want the military contract?" asked Marjorie.

"Who knows?" said Essie, "Surely it would be lucrative for the company. Maybe he has some moral objections to his company performing any sort of war business."

"That does sound like Lester," observed Opal. "He was always such a gentle soul. Every time he spoke of his company, I always remember that he discussed the beneficial products they made—things like systems for self-guiding wheelchairs. Oh! Maybe we could get Fay something like that!" Opal suddenly brightened, smiling at Fay and reaching out to give her friend's hand a squeeze.

"Whatever they produce or might produce in the future is not a question for us to worry about now," said Essie, standing up decisively. "I think it's clear from reading this codicil, that those detectives—Blake and Farley—need to see this addition to Lester's will *asap*."

"I agree," said Marjorie.

"We heard Julie's brother say that the detectives were on their way up to Lester's apartment with Felix. Maybe they're there by now. We could go check," said Essie.

"I don't know, Essie," said Opal, "That seems rather presumptuous on our parts. Why don't we just call the police station and report what we have and have them stop by like they did before?"

"Why, Opal?" argued Marjorie. "They're here at Happy Haven now. Let's go find them and give them the codicil."

"I'm with Marjorie," said Essie.

"What's your vote, Fay?" asked Marjorie, turning to their friend in her wheelchair. Fay just smiled at each of them.

"She abstains," said Essie, deadpan. "Let's go!" Essie grabbed her walker and headed towards her door. Marjorie followed, and Opal reluctantly grabbed Fay's wheelchair and brought up the rear.

The foursome zoomed through the lobby, stopping only while Essie asked Phyllis where Felix was.

"Oh, Essie," replied the cheerful clerk, "I believe he took those two detectives who are investigating Mr. Mills' accident—you know them——up to Mr. Mills' apartment. It's up on the second floor in . . ."

"Thanks, Phyllis!" shouted Essie over her shoulder as she headed for the elevator. "I know where it is!" Marjorie waved at Phyllis and Opal and Fay just smiled at her. Phyllis gave the four women a mystified little grin and then returned to her work.

Chapter 28

Essie knocked on Lester's door. Marjorie stood beside her and Opal stood behind them, to the side of Fay's wheelchair.

The door opened abruptly. Detective Blake was standing there, towering in the doorway, glaring down at the four ladies.

"What do you four want?" he asked. Farley and Felix Federico quickly scurried over to the doorway to see what was happening. They remained behind Blake.

"Detective," began Essie, the leader, "I believe we have something that you might be looking for." She held out the envelope.

"Oh?" asked Blake incredulously, but still taking the envelope. "And just what is this?"

"It's a codicil to Lester Mills' last will and testament," replied Opal from her safe position behind Essie.

"And how, may I ask, did you ladies happen upon this document?"

"Um," began Essie, "what you should be asking, Detective, is how this codicil will affect your investigation. Please, just take a look at it."

"Yes," agreed Marjorie, trying to lead the man down any path other than one that would send Essie and her friends to the hoosegow, "I think you'll find it provides ample motivation for Lester's children to plan and execute his murder."

"Oh, really?" sneered Blake.

"Yes," said Essie, "so, we'll leave you to it, Detective. Just wanted to give it to you. Let's go, girls." She turned her walker and pointed herself down the hallway.

"Just a moment!" cried Blake. "None of you are going anywhere. Farley! Bring them all inside. I want to have a little chat with these nosy little ladies." He grabbed Essie's walker, stopping her forward movement in its tracks. "Go on! Inside, all of you." He pulled on Essie's walker and gestured for the others to come inside the apartment.

Once inside, Farley motioned for the four women to be seated on Lester's sofa and arm chairs.

"Hello, Felix," said Marjorie to the manager.

"Marjorie," said Felix, nodding to her. "Opal. Fay." He acknowledged them all. "Essie, what have you been up to?"

"Excuse me, Mr. Federico," said Blake, his upraised hand stopping the manager's questions. "I'll do the questioning. "Essie, I mean, Ms. Cobb, what have you been up to?"

"We were just trying to help," squeaked out Essie with a grin. She clutched the handles of her walker that she'd placed directly in front of her, obviously for a quick getaway, if an opportunity showed itself.

The big detective opened the envelope and glanced quickly at its contents. He gestured for Farley to come over and look at the codicil.

"Where did you get this, Miss Essie?" asked Farley, shaking a loose strand of blond hair from her eyes.

"I, uh," stammered Essie. "Does it really matter? What's important is what this codicil means. This document gives Lester's children motivation to kill him. You see, Mills Electronics has been seeking and has been granted a major contract with the military and we believe Lester's children, as the acting company officers, are planning to accept that contract, even though this codicil to Lester's will clearly states that Lester himself does not want the company to accept such contracts. With their father out of the way, the children are free to sign the lucrative military contract."

"Of course," said Opal, "they ran into a problem when the rocket they aimed at him on the Fourth of July didn't kill him but only put him in the hospital. That's why they've been trying to kill him in his hospital room. If Lester were to recover and discover what had happened to him, he would surely realize that it was his children who had caused the accident and probably drum them out of the company all together."

"And I ask you ladies again," said Blake, "where did you get this addendum to Mr. Mills' will? Surely, Mills' children didn't give it to you. And I doubt Mills himself gave it to you, so that suggests that the four of you discovered it yourself in this very apartment while you were snooping."

"Oh, Detective," giggled Essie, "we told you, everyone here at Happy Haven are all friends. We're all like one big happy family. Opal here knows Lester from way back. Tell him, Opal. Tell him how you know Lester and how he invited you into his apartment and, well, tell him!"

"Miss Essie," said Felix, interrupting Essie's monologue, "you know that whenever a resident is taken ill and sent to the hospital, we always make certain their apartment is locked with the master key. I have my master key here." He held up a duplicate of the gold key that Essie had used earlier to enter the apartment. Essie grinned.

"Hmm, so you do," claimed Essie, "but Mr. Federico, when we came by earlier, I could swear Lester's door was wide open. Wasn't it, girls?"

"Oh, yes," said Marjorie.

"Totally," agreed Opal.

Fay nodded in support of her friends.

"I find that hard to believe," said Felix, glaring at the women. Then his eyes fell on Fay's sweet face and his demeanor changed. "Of course, Detective, it is *possible* that one of our workers left the door open—maybe after cleaning or something. I don't know, but I'm sure that these ladies would not lie about something so important as a resident's security, would you, ladies?"

"Oh, no," said Essie, and all of the rest said the same as they all shook their heads.

"Oh, never mind!" cried Blake, by now totally flummoxed. "It's neither here nor there. Just all of you––stay out of this room!"

"Oh, we will, Detective," said Essie, satisfied that she was now in the clear.

"We're going to have to contact Mills' attorney and see if this codicil is valid before we do anything else," said Blake. "Farley, you and I need to get over to that hospital and double check on Mr. Mills' progress and also his safety. We may need to increase our security on his room. If this military contract is at all large, I'm guessing those children are not going to stop until they've eliminated the only barrier to completing it, and that apparently is their father."

"Oh, thank you, Detective," said Opal. "I've been so worried about Lester. Please let us know how he's doing."

"You ladies just concern yourselves with staying out of trouble," said Blake, shaking his finger. "And Mr. Federico, I am holding *you* responsible for their safety and their behavior. I don't want any of them gallivanting around—here at Happy Haven and particularly not outside—causing trouble."

"Don't worry, Detective," agreed Felix. "You can count on me. It will be my honor and my duty as an

American citizen to protect these ladies. And to make sure they behave." Felix held his hand to his heart as if he were reciting the Pledge of Allegiance. Blake gave him a strange look, then gestured to Farley and they headed out the door.

"Now, ladies, remember what I said, *behave*!" said Blake as he and his partner disappeared down the hallway.

"Oh, Madre de Dios!" cried Felix after they were gone. "What a day it has been at Happy Haven. You ladies create the havoc, I think you say! And, Miss Fay! You are all mix-ed up in this fiasco! And I thought you were the little sweet one! Will Felix never learn? Let us go." He gestured for the women to exit Lester Mills' apartment and he turned and locked the apartment up with his gold master key. Then, following the women to the elevator, he escorted them down to the first floor and left them all together in Essie's room.

"Are you sure you want to leave us alone together, Felix?" Essie asked. "I mean, we might plot an escape."

"Oh, Miss Essie," Felix chuckled. "You are, as the people they say, the cards."

Off he went, laughing to himself.

Chapter 29

The next day at lunch, Essie and her friends were reviewing all that had happened in the last few days. Everyone was still sipping coffee except for Fay who was taking an inordinately long time finishing her chocolate pudding.

"Essie!" whispered Opal, "Don't look now, but those detectives are coming this way."

"Good," replied Essie, waving her hand at the two officers and another man carrying a large camera. The detectives were looking around the dining hall. When they saw Essie, they hurried over to her table. "Detectives! Have you arrested Lester Mills' children yet?"

"As a matter of fact, ladies," said Farley, with a twinkle in her eye, "we have! And we thought you all would like to know, so we stopped off here at Happy Haven to tell you."

"What about Lester?" asked Opal, her concern obviously much more centered on the father rather than his children. "Is there any improvement?" Essie worried that Opal would pull her jewel right off its chain if she didn't stop tugging it so hard.

"Actually," continued the blond officer, "you will be happy to know, Miss Opal, that Mr. Mills has regained consciousness. His doctor expects him to make a full recovery." She beamed at Opal, and Opal let loose the grasp of her necklace and sighed deeply.

"Oh, I'm so relieved," she said.

"Of course," added Blake, "he's still very groggy, so we haven't yet told him about arresting his children. . ."

"We don't want to upset him in his condition," continued Farley, "and, of course, his doctor wouldn't let us question him yet, so we still have a lot of unanswered questions . . ."

"But, Detectives," interrupted Essie, "you said you arrested the children. Did you have sufficient evidence to do so?"

"As a matter of fact," declared Blake, "we did—thanks to you, Miss Essie. Thanks to all of you ladies." He glanced around the table. All the women smiled and Fay gurgled a bit as some chocolate pudding dribbled down her chin. "After we left you yesterday, we tracked down Mr. Mills' lawyer. Of course, he couldn't or wouldn't discuss that codicil you found. He gave us that "lawyer privilege" business. Even though Mr. Mills was unconscious and critically injured, his lawyer was not willing to tell us the nature of the codicil—or even the nature of the original will. But he was willing to tell us that Mills had made an appointment a day or two earlier to come and see him about his will and that he never showed up. The lawyer had wondered why until he saw in the newspaper about Mills' injury and that he was in the hospital which explained his failure to make the appointment."

"Yes," said Farley, "but the lawyer admitted he had no idea what Mills wanted to discuss with him. I didn't get the impression that the lawyer was aware of any dissention between Mills and his children. My guess is that all of the problems arose quite recently when the children wanted this contract with the military and Mills didn't. We don't know if it was the brainchild of one of the kids or if they were all in on it together. Sometimes, good parents just have bad children."

"Did the lawyer say anything about Lester's present will?" asked Essie.

"No," said Blake, "but we assumed from much of what he said that it was a fairly standard distribution of his assets among the three children. The lawyer didn't mention anything about any family squabbles, so we're guessing that before all of this drone business, the will made for a simple three-way division among the children."

"So," reasoned Essie, "whatever changes to the will or whatever reasons caused the changes must have been recent."

"We assume so," said Blake.

"But, of course," continued Farley, "from our standpoint, the will is still a mystery. What is not a mystery and what actually led us to arresting the children is all thanks to you, Essie."

"Me?" asked Essie, delighted and bewildered.

"Yes," said Blake, "We took the earring you found in that field into evidence and were able to get a search warrant for the daughter's home and vehicle based on the possibility that it might be hers. We hadn't gone any further than the back seat of her car, when we discovered the photograph you had described that you said was hanging on Mr. Mills' wall. The earring we have perfectly matches the one Julie Mills is wearing in the photograph. Add that fact to the recent revelation that Mills' Electronics has just signed a contract with the Pentagon to build a new drone-launched missile extremely similar to the one that injured Mr. Mills, and we had sufficient evidence for the DA to sign an arrest warrant for Julie Mills and her two brothers for attempted murder."

"So the Mills siblings are in jail now?" asked Essie.

"They are," said Blake.

"Maybe you ladies would like to come out of retirement and join the Reardon Police force," suggested Farley.

"No, Detectives," said Essie, shaking her head, "I've got more than enough mysteries to solve here at Happy Haven." She glanced over at Fay, who was wiping the chocolate pudding from her face.

"Anyway," said Blake, looking over at the photographer who'd been standing patiently behind them. "Ladies, I'd like to introduce you to Phil Glasswood from the *Reardon Gazette*. He's been pestering. . . I mean asking us to do a story on you all as Farley and I told him about your sleuthing in the field and finding that earring. It's not every day that senior citizens in a retirement center break a major case of attempted murder like this . . ."

"Ladies!" greeted the man with the camera, coming up to the table. He was wearing a beige jacket and jeans. His flyaway hair and skinny neck were certainly traits one would want behind, not in front of a camera. "I'd like to get a shot of all of you if I could." He motioned for them to scoot closer together. By now, with the police and the camera man, the entire dining hall—at least the few diners remaining in it—were riveted on the little drama going on at Essie's table.

"Say *murder*!" said Essie to her pals, as they leaned in together for the shot.

"Essie!" cried Marjorie, "that's not a good word to produce a good smile. Why do you think they tell people to say *cheese*?"

"Believe me, Marjorie, I have a much more dramatic reaction to murder than I do to cheese," responded Essie.

"Now, ladies!" said Glasswood, "just hold still long enough for me to . . ."

"Good luck on this one, Glasswood," said Blake in the photographer's ear. "And remember, you asked for it." With that, Blake and Farley started out of the dining room.

"Good bye, Detectives!" cried Marjorie, waving and again disrupting the photograph.

"Hold still, miss, please!" cried Glasswood.

All of the women were now waving farewell to the detectives as the photographer tried vainly to get their attention.

Eventually the picture was taken and the cameraman had asked some pointed questions for which the women provided succinct and detailed answers.

"Sleuthing is my middle name," declared Essie.

"Essie has already solved many mysteries here at Happy Haven," added Marjorie.

"She has," confirmed Opal. "We usually help her, although I'm often reluctant to get involved."

"Not me!" said Marjorie. "I'm always up for anything exciting—if you know what I mean."

"And your friend in the wheelchair?" asked Glasswood, gesturing at Fay.

"That's Fay," said Essie. "She's mute, but she understands what's going on, and she's part of our group."

"So she's a sleuth too?" he asked.

"Yes, she is," the three speaking ladies all said.

With that, the photographer evidently had enough information and shots, so he departed, leaving the four women alone at the table—and practically alone in the dining hall. Only Santos could be seen vacuuming the rug at the far end of the room.

"My, what an exciting day!" declared Opal when they were finally all alone. "And what makes it the best day, is that Lester will recover."

"And the police have caught and arrested the criminals," said Marjorie.

"It's really too bad though," added Essie, "that the people who tried to kill Lester were his own children."

"I know," agreed Opal. "What's that famous saying? I think it's from *King Lear*. 'How sharper than a serpent's tooth it is to have a thankless child!'"

"And Lester's children were worse than thankless; they were murderous," said Essie.

Fay slapped her hands on the table.

"Is that punctuation, Fay?" asked Opal, "or are you making a statement?"

Fay just smiled and nodded.

Chapter 30

Many weeks later, Happy Haven seemed to be back to normal. Ned had reported to Essie that he had attempted to flirt with Julie Mills at a local bar but that she'd shot him down. He'd seen her drive off in a car with her two brothers. Ned had laughed that *all* of his endeavors at Mills Electronics had not been successful. He felt vindicated that Julie had been arrested. Truth be told, Essie was glad that Ned hadn't gotten anywhere romantically with the murderous Julie—he was safer that way.

Now it was evening and the four ladies were again sipping their after dinner coffee in the crowded dining hall. A smattering of applause filled the air, and all four turned to look up at the entrance to see Lester Mills, leaning on a crutch, walking into the room.

"Oh, my!" cried Opal. "Lester's back!"

"Don't just sit there, Opal," urged Marjorie. "You know you want to go talk to him."

"That would be presumptuous. I think I'd better just stay here and . . ."

But Lester had himself noticed the four women— Opal in particular—and he was headed in their direction, limping slowly.

"Opal!" he said as he finally reached their table. "You're looking just as lovely as you did the last time I saw you."

"Oh, Lester," replied Opal, blushing.

"Mr. Mills," spoke up Essie, attempting to put an end to any lovey dovey talk, "we're glad to see you back and well."

"All thanks to you, I understand, Miss Essie," said Lester with a one-handed salute.

"Well, I believe I owe the results of my sleuthing efforts to you," declared Essie firmly. "After all, you did save my life. If you hadn't jumped on me—so they tell me—that rocket would have plowed right into the back of my head."

"I was happy to serve as your guardian, ma'am," he said with a twinkle in his eye. Then immediately, he turned back to Opal. "And, Opal, I am so relieved that you were not injured that evening, what with all the horrible mischief that my children perpetrated that night. It's a wonder that I was the only person affected. That drone rocket could have maimed or killed a lot of Happy Haven residents if it had landed just slightly farther to one side or another."

"We're so sorry to hear about your children, Lester," said Opal, her eyes filling with tears. "I never had children, but I simply cannot imagine how devastated you must be . . ."

"I'm just happy that their mother never lived to see what became of them," Lester mused, looking solemnly, his head bowed. "She was such a gentle soul. This would surely have killed her."

"And you?" asked Opal. "How are you handling it?" She touched his hand lightly, her face filled with tenderness.

"To tell the truth, Opal," he said sadly, "I lost those kids long ago. They were always more interested in making money than in making the world a better place. That's why I went into engineering in the first place—I believed in science; I believed—and still do—that science can help improve our lives and the world we live in, but my children—all three of them—only saw the company as a way to make money, and the more the better. I mean, if they really believed in our drone's military applications as a means to help the government protect our country, it would be one thing. But they don't. They only care about money. They were the ones who were promoting this military drone rocket; they'd been keen on it for years, but I had opposed it and we'd been arguing about it right up until the day I officially retired. I thought when I handed the reins over to James that we'd finally agreed *not* to pursue the military contract, but I was wrong. The minute I left, they turned around and went against me, signing that contract for that drone that they were developing all along, right under my nose."

"What are you going to do now?" asked Essie.

"I don't know," he said. "Everything is on hold at the company now. I'm really just not able to continue running things there—particularly now." He gestured to his crutch and bandages. "I have a nephew who works for me and whom I believe shares my vision and I'm thinking of bringing him on board to run things for a while. If he works out, I may hand the reins over to him permanently."

"And your children?" asked Marjorie.

"Well, they're my children and I'll always love them, but I certainly don't like them very much, not after everything they've done," Lester said squeezing his mouth together and shaking his head. "Even so, I've gotten them all good lawyers and that's about all I can do. This is a case of attempted murder, not just some family squabble. There's only so much I can do for them now. They made their bed, and so forth."

"Oh, Lester," whispered Opal with a sigh. "I'm so sorry for you."

"Oh, don't be too sorry," replied Lester, "I may have lost my children, but I've gained a dear old friend." He patted Opal's hand fondly. "I'm not at all sorry to be leaving Mills Electronics. Happy Haven holds great promise for me. And, I understand that the four of you ladies outdid yourselves in helping the police solve this mystery."

"It was mostly Essie's doing," said Opal.

"It usually is," added Marjorie. "We just help." She gave the silver-haired Lester a flirtatious smile.

"I appreciate it, ladies, more than I can say," he replied to them all. "Hopefully now, everything will calm down."

As he said *calm down*, the loud-speaker system in the dining hall came alive with some bouncy music. Everyone looked around to see what was going on. One lady at a center table wearing a bright red jump suit stood up suddenly and strode over to the center of the room.

"For all you men!" she announced. The music pulsated. The tune was catchy and familiar—"I Am Woman, Hear Me Roar." The lady in red gyrated around a few steps and then was immediately joined by two other women from more distant tables who mimicked her moves exactly. Then several more were added and then even more.

"Sorry, Lester," said Opal, patting his hand with a coy smile, "things won't be getting calm just yet."

"Let's go, gals!" cried Essie as she stood up, grabbed her walker and led the other three (with Opal pushing Fay's wheelchair) into the middle of the room with the other women.

The music built and the audience of men clapped with wild abandon, canes and walker legs pounding on the floor.

"Go, girls, go!" shouted the octogenarians and nonagenarians. The ladies dancing in the middle of the room responded to the encouragement and kicked up heels and discreetly pulled up hems to entice their all-male audience. Soon everyone from the kitchen and the staff had gathered at the entrances, clapping in time to the music.

When the music finally reached its crescendo, the ladies formed their final pose to thunderous applause. After the dance, Essie rolled back to her table along with Marjorie, Opal and Fay.

"Ladies," said Lester Mills, who was still standing there, "that was the best dance routine I've ever seen! You four are amazing!"

"We were, weren't we?" agreed Marjorie.

Felix Federico, who'd been watching the entire routine from the main entrance, was going around to all the tables congratulating the participants.

"Magnifico! Bravo!" he said, touching each woman as he rounded all the tables. Finally, he arrived at Essie's table. "Oh, you ladies! You are, as they say, the pajamas of the cat!" He moved around the table, tapping each woman's shoulder in praise. When he reached Fay's wheelchair, he kneeled down and gave Fay a long, warm embrace. Opal, somewhat aghast at the manager's rather open affection for her special charge, became annoyed.

"Excuse me, Mr. Federico," she said, interrupting Felix's embrace with Fay. "I can't help but think that you're being just a bit too intimate with Fay. I mean, just because she doesn't speak, doesn't mean you can take advantage of her . . ."

"Take advantage?" he cried, standing up abruptly. "Oh, Miss Opal, I never do such a thing. Miss Fay is very dear lady. I never harm her. I care for her just as I care for my sister."

"What does your sister have to do with anything?" demanded Opal.

"You see," he began, "I have a sister who is much like Fay. Rosa, my oldest sister. For many years when we were children, she was like all of us—her brothers and sisters. Then one day, just like you told me about Fay, she stopped speaking. We tried everything to get Rosa to speak. We know she understands, but she cannot speak. For many years, this goes on. But all that time, we always treat Rosa with love and care and we all talk to her as *if* she can speak and if we expect her to speak any day. Then, one day, not long ago, Rosa—she began to speak. We never knew why. We never knew why she stopped speaking. We never knew why she started again. We just kept loving her and talking to her. She does not speak a lot, but now she does speak. I believe Miss Fay is very much like my sister Rosa and I hope that she too will speak again. Until then, I will do for her like I always did for my sister Rosa. I don't know if it will help, but I hope that it will."

"Oh, Felix," said Marjorie. "That is beautiful."

"I feel ashamed that I have not been doing that myself," said Opal. "After all, I am with Fay all the time. She *is* my charge."

"Do not feel bad, Miss Opal," said Felix. "You could not have known about my sister. Miss Fay, she loves you. She knows how much you love her and take care of her."

"I agree," said Lester, piping in. "Opal, no one could ever doubt your loving nature. In just the short time I've been here at Happy Haven, I can see how tender-hearted you are. Your concern for your friend here and how you include her in everything—how all three of you ladies include her in everything—is just one example to me of what genuinely nice people you all are. You ladies are the total opposite of my heartless children." He smiled weakly and a tear formed in his eye.

Fay looked up at Lester's face and reached out her hand to grab his. She squeezed it and smiled.

"I don't think I've ever seen Fay do that with anyone other than the three of us," observed Essie.

"I tell you, lovely ladies," said Felix, beaming at the little lady in the wheelchair, "Miss Fay is just full of love. When she finally decides to speak—everyone had better watch out the below!"

At that, everyone laughed, including Fay.

THE END

ABOUT THE AUTHOR

 Patricia Rockwell is the author of two mystery series. Her Pamela Barnes acoustic mysteries include *Sounds of Murder*, *FM For Murder*, *Voice Mail Murder*, *Stump Speech Murder*, and *Murder in the Round*. Her Essie Cobb senior sleuth mysteries include *Bingoed*, *Papoosed*, *Valentined*, and *Ghosted*. She is the founder and publisher of Cozy Cat Press, which specializes in producing cozy (or gentle) mysteries.

Dr. Rockwell is presently living in Aurora, Illinois, with her husband Milt, also a retired educator.